WHAT PEOPLE ARE SAYING ABOUT

SUBLIMINAL MESSIAH

Subliminal Messiah is a hypnotic black comedy wrapped in a surreal vision quest dipped in the grotesque. A story of love and destiny, hope and fear, Jacques has created a modern day Don Quixote in Ezekiel Downs, and surrounded him with a cast of misfits and delinquents.

Richard Thomas, *Staring Into the Abyss*

Continuing to cough up his superb prose with pace, Jacques here kicks hard on the accelerator to unveil a stripped-back literary fiction in a polished up hot rod—featuring a desperate man named Ezekiel pinned to the wheel, odds against him, cruising in search of a saviour.

Andrez Bergen, *One Hundred Years of Vicissitude*

Anthony David Jacques takes the clairvoyant anti-hero trope and brings it to the world of barhopping, horserace-gambling vagabonds. Jacques has created a story that unabashedly praises nihilism without devolving into simple cynicism; he is an author who is not afraid to let his characters discuss death in a way that lacks the romanticized baggage of much contemporary story-telling. *Subliminal Messiah's* Ezekiel, the unlucky psychic, is *Fight Club's* unnamed narrator; each living in a perpetual mental haze which readers will eagerly navigate to the final page.

Caleb J. Ross, *Stranger Will*

T0340920

Subliminal Messiah

By Ezekiel Downs

Collected and compiled by

Anthony David Jacques

Subliminal Messiah

By Ezekiel Downs

Collected and compiled by

Anthony David Jacques

PERFECT
EDGE
BOOKS

Winchester, UK
Washington, USA

First published by Perfect Edge Books, 2014
Perfect Edge Books is an imprint of John Hunt Publishing Ltd., Laurel House, Station Approach,
Alresford, Hants, SO24 9JH, UK
office1@jhpbooks.net
www.johnhuntpublishing.com
www.perfectedgebooks.com

For distributor details and how to order please visit the 'Ordering' section on our website.

Text copyright: Anthony David Jacques 2013

ISBN: 978 1 78099 483 3

A CIP catalogue record for this book is available from the British Library.

Design: Stuart Davies

Printed and bound by CPI Group (UK) Ltd, Croydon, CR0 4YY

We operate a distinctive and ethical publishing philosophy in all
areas of our business, from our global network of authors to
production and worldwide distribution.

I must extend a special thanks to my exceptionally patient wife, Julia, and my unbearably lovely daughter, Adelaide. Without the hours I stole away from the two of you, this project would have never had a chance.

And in no particular order, I would be remiss if I failed to mention: Phil Jourdan, Mark Vanderpool, Jason Heim, Richard Thomas, Caleb J. Ross, Michael P. Gonzalez, Edward J. Rathke, Nik Korpon, Chris Deal, Gordon Highland, Simon West-Bulford, Dr. Schwerkoske and his amazing team, anyone else from The Cult, The Velvet or Write Club who ever looked at this mess without running away, and of course, all of the many endless, dreamless nights.

0:

A light swings above my head, slowly arcing into an oval that grows smaller and smaller the way you'd imagine a star collapsing into a black hole. Shadows creep around eight square feet of concrete, my garden-level worm's-eye view of the world. And to think, I've been sleeping a good six feet under the last couple years already. Irony is knowing that tomorrow I can't be any more dead than I am right now. The main difference is breathing.

Memories move with the ebb and flow of the darkness, hide the moment you need them, shy away like ghosts from the light. I've never put so much effort into remembering the past until tonight. Can't help but wonder where I went wrong. Every time the light stops swinging I pull the switch off and savor the flash of blindness, uncertainty.

Pull the light on and pick up a pen.

Everything is now.

This thought crowds my mind with relentless urgency, pushes everything else away and I can't sleep and I can't dream and still this girl dances on the edges of my consciousness while I sit staring at an almost blank page. Our fateful encounter, chatting innocently over coffee before every element of our little dream world comes loose and everything fades to white, and then I wake up, one day closer to today.

My face tingles, half from bruises and half from the coffee grounds stuffed into my lower lip like a plug of tobacco. Hardly able to hold steady enough to write, the side of my hand leaves little toe-less footprints that get lighter and lighter as the grated flesh begins to clot, and right now I've got to fill in the gaps. With so many notebooks missing, I've got to connect the pieces here and now to make it coherent if for no other reason, to finally finish something.

By now I realize writing things down hasn't done me any good, so I suppose I've done this for you. So, for what it's worth, you're welcome. Welcome to the end of my life, because the truth is I messed up. I got it wrong. I brought this on myself, and through it all I end up feeling blindsided.

If you're reading this, odds are I'm dead, and I know a lot about odds. I'm a ninety-nine to one underdog at best. But, if what you're reading happens to be printed, if it's set in ten- or twelve-point Times New Roman or Arial, Courier New or Helvetica instead of chicken scratch in a red spiral notebook, then at least I got it done. It wouldn't be worth publishing without an ending, so if this is more than just a stack of college-ruled paper then at least I finally finished something I started. I haven't totally died in vain.

If you're reading this now, it's probably been edited for grammar, punctuation, maybe content. It's probably been stream-lined to make a good story arc, but it's all true, and if I'm lucky I'll get it all out before my pacing shadow wears a hole in the thinning carpet and I fall into the big black hole of fading memories. And somehow I can't even think where to start. Nine years; I had everything laid out for me and it's come down to this.

Right now, in this actual moment of real tangible time, I can't tell you how this is going to end. All I can tell you is how I got here, hunched over another notebook, scribbling out my life and unable to trust anyone with it.

And then there's Mona. Mona. Mona. Her name is a mantra deep inside my chest. She's out there right now, Mona, and Eddie, and even my deadbeat, bankrupt millionaire of a father. It's about to turn from really late into awfully early, so they're likely sleeping, dreaming away the previous day, all sailing toward the inevitable. But here I sit, face to face, once again, with my inability to change anything.

Now I am somewhere I am not supposed to be
And I can see things I know I really shouldn't see

PART I

And now I know why, and now I know why
Things aren't as pretty on the inside

1:

I'll start with people I hate. Allison tops that list because she's just given herself a clever new nickname, Lissa. She's been at this as long as I've known her, replacing names almost as often as boyfriends, which is an easy transition to spot.

Nobody here ever meets the guys she dates, but it's easy to tell what they're like. For the last one, Ally (her previous nom du jour) became a European post-punk fashion spread. She knew nothing about The Dead Kennedys or The Clash, but she found her way into a whole new wardrobe of brand new purple or black jeans with ripped knees and stress marks, a leather jacket covered in rock-band-esque patches, weathered black boots and a metal studded belt. This is how a fashion house re-invents the dark side of the eighties and sells it for eight hundred bucks an outfit.

She's half the reason I stopped wearing my ages-old ripped jeans and leather jacket, because I know all about guilt-by-association and we worked the same shifts an awful lot. I held on to my concert shirts like any other audiophile, but tossed that studded leather belt into the trash. It was half duct-taped together anyway.

Then something must have happened. About a month ago she dyed her hair back to a normal shade, stopped going by Ally, ditched the jeans and boots in favor of her typical club-hopper look and started bouncing around the coffee shop with her heaving cleavage screaming, "Hey, boys, I'm back on the market."

Last week it began again with the research: Aerosmith, The Stones, The Doors, The Who. I'd be happy for anyone else going through this kind of renaissance with classic rock, but for Allison (ahem, Lissa) it means she's found a new victim.

Now she's shown up to work squeezed into a Led Zeppelin

baby doll and cut-off jean shorts, and her hair says she hasn't been home at all the night before. She pulls out a stack of CDs and begins shuffling through them while I get the shop ready.

"I love all the pictures on the album covers. They're so weird, and all the bright colors are so...oh dammit, I got ripped off. This one's blank." She holds it up, but I know it without looking.

"White Album. Beatles." I mean, who doesn't know that?

"Oh yeah. Weird, you totally read my mind."

"And it was just as blank."

"Huh?"

"Just put something in."

"Whatever."

By the time our OPEN sign flickers on she's skipped her way through a dozen albums. I'm trying to take orders when the music pauses and she asks what 'In-A-Gadda-Da-Vida' means, but the opening chords rumble out of the speakers before I can answer and now she's bobbing her head, smacking her gum, wiggling around likes it's some sort of Iron Butterfly meets Madonna dance remix.

This old man turns rash red trying to make himself audible over the stereo and I finally grab the remote from her and start clicking away at the volume right in time to hear the bell ring on the shop's door.

"A bit loud, don't you think?"

David. He's easy to hate, because no matter how cool someone is outside of work, everyone learns to hate the man who signs their paycheck.

David owns Gallagher's, a "friendly, neighborhood coffee shop tucked snugly into the first floor of a multi-unit apartment building in the heart of downtown Minneapolis", according to the Pioneer Press. More like stuck directly in the cross hairs of a T-intersection. What the reviews never mention is that the afternoon sun fills the entire shop with blinding light. If you think David would spend one dime on window shades, you think too highly of the man.

But Gallagher's is a bit of an oasis nonetheless. It's a couple blocks east of a tiny university, a couple blocks south of the stadium, a good six blocks north of the bad part of town. In business terms, this means you've got college kids to carry your profit margin through the school year, sporadic bursts of business from sports fans, and an abundance of Somalis (Minneapolis, for some reason, has an enormous Somali population) who live right upstairs and all around and happen to love coffee. And look, there's a tiny slice of grass and trees right across the street.

I work the early shift because I roast the coffee. David paid to have 'Roasted Fresh Every Morning' as our official slogan because that's what we do. Halfway up the butt crack of dawn I pull myself out of bed to get the day's roast going. I take the green coffee beans from these fifty-pound bags labeled Guatemala, Peru, Tanzanian Pea Berry and Sumatra; I transform them into Full City Roast, Vienna Roast, French Roast or Espresso.

And I mean early. I haven't physically seen a sunrise in over a year. When the sun does come up, it blinds me along with a few unlucky patrons for about ten minutes as it reflects off the zillion-faceted steel, glass and concrete monstrosity of skyline we call Minneapolis. The Pioneer Press review doesn't mention that either. The blinding light crashes in through the floor-to-ceiling window as I stand hostage in front of the roaster, but it's all worth it.

If I know one thing, it's that my mystery girl loves coffee, and that's why I work here. I've learned everything there is to know about coffee, because you have to start somewhere.

And now, the clock reads eight-fourteen in the AM and my break is almost over. The clock says, *It's already another fourteen minutes closer to the end, so thanks for sharing but you should get back to work before Allison/Ally/Elise/Lissa breaks all the mugs.*

I rub the exhaustion from my face and head to the front of the shop, where everything is still warm from the morning's roast, and pour myself a warm cup of Tanzania.

"I chipped another nail, dammit." She doesn't even look at me when she talks. "These aren't cheap. Oh, and another mug bit the dust. You should finish the dishes while I count the tips, cool?"

2:

A collection of thrift-store-reject furniture huddles around an enormous seventies-style television. You know the type; shaped like a bulky end table with a door that closes over the screen and a six-button remote the size of a brick. Top of the line, twenty-five years ago.

Odd colors splash sporadically against the opposing wall, silhouetting a man as he dozes on an uneven love seat. Every few minutes he rustles half-awake and by second-nature flips to the next channel.

—right folks! There's only a few of these incredible Wonder-Matic blenders left. Boy I don't think these will last another—

The room has the tepid reek of a stale refrigerator left open for a week inside a smoky laundromat. Empty cans of Tab and Diet Pepsi are scattered around plastic cafeteria-style plates to which several weeks of leftovers are fossilized. He wakes, stirs, and flips to the next channel.

—Holy cow, Bob! Look at the size of that catfish. Man, that'll be good eats! Tell you what, these new wiggly-jigs—

From the looks of things inside, the smell, you'd think this family was on the skids, ready to crumble under the pressure of both parents working a handful of part-time jobs, juggling food stamps and welfare, hardly able to afford school supplies.

This man, swaddled unconscious in ragged sweat pants and an over-stretched wife-beater, sunken into the decrepit couch; this was the same man who neighbors saw power-washing his driveway every other weekend. Driving his lovely wife and rambunctious kids to church every Sunday. Neighbors had no suspicion of the self-imposed squalor we endured just inside those walls. Dad, another person I've never liked, he rustles, flips to the next channel.

—use some hunter green now, and put a lovely little birch tree right

there, peeking out of the fog. A happy birch tree—

The house is large without looking imposing, roomy enough for the average family. Newly remodeled, fresh paint, the picket fence white and clean; the lawn, a deep Kentucky bluish-green and landscaping that bordered on being called manicured, yet simple and neat. Two impressively clean, liquid shiny late-model cars sit in the drive, and even the planter around the mailbox is just right. It's all part of the illusion.

He gurgles, snorts, flips to the next channel.

—OK! No credit? OK! Bankruptcy? OK! Divorce? OK! Call now for your pre-approved loan! Don't let your creditors keep hassling—

Anyone who saw this man mowing his yard or trimming the hedgerow along the drive would think of him as kind and hardworking, habitual and disciplined, a family man. They would assume they only ever saw him in baggy sweat pants because that's what he wore for yard work. They'd figure he had at least a half-dozen suits inside a roomy walk-in closet tucked away between the master bedroom and a spacious bath.

Oh, he had the suits. It was more a question of how often he wore them. He didn't have an office to go to five days a week like a normal person. No desk, no salary, not even a clock to punch. The suits, they were his Sunday best.

The hand holding the remote jolts and the TV flips to the NASA Channel, the room now bathed in the soft glow of a pale blue dot against a stark black background speckled with stars. The bottom corner of the screen says Live Feed. The only sound is the cathode ray tube in the back of the TV set, that annoying pitch right at the top of the human auditory range.

Neighbors assumed that since they never actually saw him going to work he must be an early riser. He must get home late. His boys were building a fort in the back yard and his wife took care of a small garden and tended the flowers. Neighbors had no idea this was his second wife. No idea that the boys were only half-brothers that hated this thin candy-shell of a life.

Outside, it was a postcard for the American dream. Inside, smoke from the man's last cigarette hung bluish grey in the air, swirling, threatening me for staying up past my bedtime, but I have trouble sleeping. As usual, I'm peeking around the corner of the hall, watching the channels change over my father's shoulder. This has become a ritual, counting up through the infomercials and the public television, waiting for Joanne to get home.

He rustles. Flips again.

—*Static; a face, eyes closed, a bottle of something, more static, a shower head, a bare foot, a house in the dark, lighted window, more static, a breast, hands over a screaming mouth, then static...*

I couldn't sleep because every time I did all I dreamed were flashes of human suffering and chaos. Night after night I was afraid to close my eyes and since Dad was the fatherly equivalent of an appendix—seemingly useless with the small possibility that he could self-destruct at any moment and take all of us out with him—that meant I had to wait for my step-mom to get home, which would be late. PTA meetings and other school stuff, she said.

This was back before any real counseling, before briefly attempting to try this or that support group or anything like that. Back when I would still zone out in the middle of class or during dinner for a couple seconds while being bombarded with a torrent of silent images. Third grade is when the first episode took place.

It felt like hours to me, but people would say it looked like I had been stunned one moment, like I had suddenly frozen in place, and the next moment I'd slump over.

In that flash of an instant I'd watch buildings burn and cars crash, limbs and faces distort and things worse than death, and always at the end, ready to usher me back to reality was this woman, the one constant in my life.

Long dark hair, straight and smooth and infinite, beyond

which there was a light that moved in calming waves, pushing me back to the present. Her lips moved as her eyes held mine and even though I could hear nothing I knew she was speaking to me, and not talking down to a third grader with attention problems or meager people skills. She was speaking to something deep within. Then fade to white and I'd rocket back to reality in time to feel the ache of having just hit the ground. I'd come to, completely disoriented, lying somewhere surrounded by concerned onlookers or classmates.

About two weeks into the third grade, I had my first vision. I came to on the playgroud, covered in vomit. Lost and scared and confused. My teacher thought it was a seizure, and they became common for a while. Sometimes I would wake up having wet myself, or maybe I'd cut my head open on a desk on the way down.

"He's just having another seizure, God dammit," she'd say.

The school nurse concurred. "Loss of bowel control. Dilated pupils. Disorientation. A classic seizure."

They'd say, "Let's get you cleaned up."

In those moments, those flashes when I'd rip through the seams of time and everything went silent, well, for a nine-year-old that's a pretty crazy thing to wrap your head around. Without the woman there at the end, I may have lost my mind.

That first time, I watched over and over as this kid fell from the school's aging jungle gym, a maze of metal bars and wooden supports. Bolts sticking out everywhere, splinters in search of loose clothing or exposed skin. Looking back, it was a lawsuit waiting to happen.

I watched him fall maybe six or eight feet from the top, the part you weren't really supposed to climb on, he slipped and took a swan dive headlong towards the pavement. This was before playgrounds used that rubbery stuff to cover the ground. There weren't even wood chips or gravel to look forward to as he sailed toward the unforgiving blacktop.

He caught himself with his hands and his right arm broke, both bones in his forearm stabbed out through his skin past either side of his elbow and then whack, his face met the asphalt. For a moment he lay there with his arm skin folded up like an accordion, eyes squeezed shut. Then he began flopping around on the ground, mouth gaping, his right cheekbone collapsed and hollow. His eyes shot wide open, clouding and distant, like a stunned fish out of water. All in complete and total silence.

And then it happened again. He fell, his arm split, the flesh cinched up, his face half-collapsed and he writhed, flopping his useless arm around. Over and over, an instant replay like all the reality shows they have now, home videos of terrible accidents and personal injuries, car crashes and people catching fire.

When I came back to reality, the change of setting from the playground back into the classroom, from future to present, was so sudden I couldn't help but vomit. I ended up soaked in my own half-digested breakfast before I had the presence of mind to try and stand. Kids all huddled around me, shrieking, and my third-grade teacher jiggled over impatiently asking, "What now?"

Mrs. Fiore. Now here's someone I flat out hated. Everyone called her Mrs. Fury for two very good reasons. First, no third-grader could pronounce Fiore in proper Italian. Second, and much more importantly, she had a mammoth temper and the maternal instinct of a black widow. Mrs. Fury. The name fit.

After a couple of these, she suggested (to anyone she felt like complaining to) that really, I ought to bring a change of clothes in my backpack and look into controlling my episodes with medication. The school nurse concurred.

For the next few months the episodes were intense, day or night, at home or at school. If it didn't happen while I was awake I was afraid to fall asleep, and if I slept well a couple nights in a row, I knew I was due. One way or another, it would come.

Kids would say, "Hey, look at me," and then they'd flop

themselves down. In the lunchroom they'd get a mouthful of milk and spew it out dramatically, shouting, "Hey, I'm Ezekiel."

Bleeeeeccchhh.

They'd chant, "Ezekiel Downs falls down." This went on for weeks, and Mrs. Fiore only stepped in when she was done covering her own laughter.

* * *

Right before Halloween everything changed. That kid really did fall. I stood there and watched him as his arm split like a piece of firewood, only this time, right after his cheek collapsed and his grand-canyon mouth ripped open, this shrill, prepubescent scream enveloped me as it echoed off the walls of the school and the playground. The chill of October faded. My hair stood on end and I began to sweat little beads of ice.

Just then, my arms tensed for the fall, but it never happened; I was awake. In that moment of real tangible time I knew the kid's parents were going to win their lawsuit, even though I hardly knew what a lawsuit was. I could see the headlines as they sued the school district for what their lawyer called 'abhorrently unsafe playground equipment'. This lawsuit would spark years of playground equipment reform.

That was the first day I started journaling. That was the first day I realized the future had no sound. By now I figure it's something like how a blind man often has a great sense of hearing or smell. By losing one sense the others tend to get stronger. With these visions, all I ever get is the sight part, no sound or touch or smell or anything. Since I only get one of the five senses, it's overwhelming. It makes real life seem fake and boring; like a bad sitcom where you see every punchline a mile away.

I see all the minute details, though at first I couldn't make sense of most of them. I watched that kid's arm break, for real, and then I saw it all healed up and how his bones had to be bolted together and he can't rotate his arm but the scar really turned out nicely, or so everyone tells him. Will tell him. I can't always be sure of things like 'when'. Then at some point he's older and he's got a tattoo around the scar, to prove that he's conquered pain. He plays bass in a band and he drives a Camaro with flames. Doctors rebuilt his cheekbone but he'll always have scars, and when he's older he tells people he earned them as a boxer, a bullfighter, a stunt man; he gets a laugh and hopes they look past it.

Getting people to look past my difficulties, however, was a tall order because at age nine it's not exactly cool to pass out and soil your pants on a somewhat regular basis. It wasn't much of a stretch for kids to think I was retarded or crazy. But when that kid really fell, my outlook on life changed. I grew up pretty damn fast that year.

I grabbed a red spiral notebook and made my first journal entry about how his arm would heal and how his parents would sue and how I wasn't sure who I should tell about all this. When more dreams came, I recorded them in my best nine-year-old handwriting because I wasn't sure what else to do. I was watching pain and misery, and sometimes these dreams were of people's final moments on God's green earth. Now, at eighteen going on dead, it seems pretty clear that was my midlife crisis.

But then there's Mona, my music-loving, coffee-drinking, chess-playing muse. She's always been there to guide me back to the present. At the end of every vision I've ever had, I've caught at least a glimpse of Mona. With her I felt an immediate sense of trust. It was effortless. The only other woman I ever tried to trust with all this was Joanne.

I stood for hours watching the late, late, late whatever show over my father's shoulder, night after night, waiting for my step-mom to finally get home and sing me to sleep, hoping she could somehow hold off these nightmares if only for a few minutes.

Every night I hoped to muster the courage to show her my little red spiral notebook, and every night I was content to cry silently on her shoulder.

I needed so bad to make sure at least one person knew I wasn't crazy. Most nights I went to bed when the static became too much to bear, until one night I dreamed of fire and I knew I was going to be alone soon.

3:

Another person I hated in the third grade: Bradon Hildegard. He was one of the few I got to pick on because no matter how retarded people thought I was with my episodes, this kid seemed to go out of his way to make himself a target. I needed so badly not to be on the bottom of the social pecking-order, he became my means to an end. I'm not proud of the way I treated him, or quite a few other kids as the years went by, but it was survival of the fittest and my only defense was a heartless offense.

I'd always mess with him during show and tell. Whatever you wanted to bring, it had to fit in a brown paper bag.

"Yeah, yeah, yeah. I've got Jesus right here," I dangled the crucifix that hung around my neck.

"That's not funny, Ezekiel. Now go ahead Bradon."

"Okay..."

"I'm not kidding. Found him under a bench in Elliot Park."

"One more outburst like that young man..."

"Hey, he's the one that brought an empty paper bag for show and tell."

"Bradon..."

"Okay," he says, eyes down, holding his empty bag. "He's not really in the bag. But he's inside my heart. I guess that's all I have to say anyway."

"Alright then. Who would like to go next?"

I raise my hand.

"Anyone?"

"What the fuck? I got my hand up?"

"That's it, young man!" She's stabbing those breakfast-link fingers toward the utility closet, her tapioca arm fat jiggling violently.

"You know it's not nice to point."

"March!"

Stab, stab, stab.

"I know, I know."

There I go, past all the kids with their Christmas sweaters, all the good little boys and girls staring at me, the problem child. Waiting for me to have another episode so they can all laugh while Mrs. Fury begrudgingly helps me get all cleaned up and into a new change of clothes. It's been so long and I still remember my little sweater with the bright red racecar on it. The one Joanne knitted for me. I hated it, but it was the closest thing I had to a Christmas sweater.

The gold star of achievement board is done up in light blue with white crepe paper trim, to look like icicles. There aren't any gold stars next to my name, only green sad-faces, like the Mr. Yuck stickers you see on household cleaners. Those represent the number of days I've ended up in the utility closet.

Each grade had two classes and the rooms were arranged like an L, joined by a door-less utility closet which was full of indoor-recess games, books and encyclopedias, extra desks all stacked up. This one had a desk and chair for me with a little hanging light.

Back with all the supplies and inside-recess games I'm supposed to think about not talking out of turn, not swearing. I sat day after day reading and re-reading the instructions to chess, because you have to start somewhere.

Really, though, I'm back here because Mrs. Fury has no patience. I overheard her telling another teacher, "It's not like I work in a nursery. I shouldn't have to be cleaning up after some retarded kid shitting his pants twice a week." So I sit in the utility closet a few days a week, more when she's feeling stressed, the light swinging side to side above my head. I pull the cord to switch it off.

Half-light. Like the night I watched the fire a thousand times. Stupid Bradon. What he didn't know was about to change his life permanently. And mine. I pull the light on again, it swings and my shadow paces, biding my time.

* * *

Christmas passes, the next semester follows in much the same manner; passing out, soiling myself, spending the rest of the day in the utility closet. Out of sight, out of mind. One day about a month before the semester is over Mrs. Fury has something to say, it's very important, so I start making fart noises under my arm. For the record, I already knew Bradon was dead.

"Quiet down, young man. This is serious!"

I shrug.

"Children, last night there was an accident and, well," she pauses dramatically, "Bradon Hildegard's house caught fire."

"Don't you mean, burned down to nothing?"

She ignores me and goes on. "I'm afraid that nobody got out of the house, children."

Boring.

"And that means that Bradon won't be with us anymore."

I ask, "What about Joanne? How's she doing?"

Her hand goes to her mouth. "Joanne?" True shock.

"You know, my step-mom. You think she made it out?"

Course, I already know.

"Ezekiel I... Wh... Do you know for sure that she was..."

"Yeah, whatever. They were having a 'PTA meeting'." I make quotes with my little third-grade fingers, should have been too young to understand those things.

"Oh, Ezekiel. I had no idea. Are you—"

"It was a pretty regular thing."

Her face almost convinces me that she is capable of a real, human emotion, but this is just shock, not sympathy or empathy or anything which might put me in her good graces for more than the afternoon.

"I'm so sorry."

"Don't bother, she deserved it."

And then her face drops. Golden.

"You heard me."

"Well, my word..."

"Your word?" I stand at my desk. "What IS your word? You say that so often, you'd think you'd decide on one already. There's Fuck, Shit, Piss."

All that stress, watching people die every night, had to let it out once in a while.

Her chubby arm stab, stab, stabs and I march to the utility closet again. Past the kids who don't even look at me anymore. Past the gold star of achievement board, now done up with eggs and rabbits even though it's way past Easter. It was downhill from there for a while, spent three or four days a week out of sight until right before the end of the year.

* * *

Mr. Jepson always acts like he's glad to see me. He hands me a test to see if I need a different kind of teacher, saying I'm special and that those other kids may not understand. Of course I know this is all about the fact that I'm about to flunk and Mrs. Fiore can't take another year of me, and no other teacher seems all that interested. Amazing what you can overhear from the waiting room outside the counselor's office. If they can put me in with the special needs kids, they can pass me with lower standards and then it's on to the fourth grade.

So Mr. Jepsen says things like, *I'm here to help.* His face marks concern, genuine interest. His smile says we're already buddies. *And how does that make you feel?*

"Ezekiel?"

"What?"

"How does that make you feel?"

"About Bradon? I didn't like him anyway. He deserved it,

along with everyone else in that house."

"Does your father know that's how you feel?"

"You think he'd disagree?"

"Mm-hm, mm-hm." He nods, pretending to listen, pretending to write in his yellow legal pad.

"Well, over the summer, your father thinks you and I should continue to see each other. You'll probably be here for summer school anyway. How do you feel about that?"

I shrug.

"It would mean a little less time in class."

Another shrug.

He says losing loved ones is hard on a child, and often children that go through tragedies act up in class the way I have been.

"Yeah, well, they weren't loved ones."

He nods as if I agreed with anything he just said.

"You're really a classic case."

"If you were a decent counselor you wouldn't be working in a grade school."

He nods, tilts his head as if to say, *Go on, let it all out.*

"Sometimes I play with my dad's guns. I pretend to shoot him in his sleep."

I could say whatever I wanted, but even that gets boring after a while. He continued to nod, eyes on his legal pad. I wait until he notices I'm no longer talking. It takes a minute.

"Well, uh...Ezekiel—can we call you Zeek?—the real tragedy here is that you won't open up, to me or anyone else."

"You want tragedy, come by Fury's class tomorrow afternoon."

"Are you planning a prank for the last day of class?"

That piqued his interest. I shrug, slouch back into my chair, and now he mirrors my body language. Finally paying attention.

"We can't help you if you won't talk, Zeek."

"You want tragedy? Keep fooling around with your

daughter's high-school friends."

I'm back in the closet before the story even gets good. I should have been too young to understand those things, but you grow up fast in the presence of death. That blonde girl reaching over, below the steering wheel, reaching lower, then her shoulders jerking, then her blonde ponytail bobbing up and down, then his foot hits the gas instead of the brake and they sail through a busy intersection. And the poor kid in the crosswalk, there's the real tragedy.

I flick the light on, send it swinging and my shadow dances while a thunderhead of potential builds, hovering thick and heavy and black over my head. Under the pacing light I give my shadow horns, they grow and shrink, longer and shorter, dancing around the utitlity closet and I lean over to see the clock. Still waiting. I've leaned over to see the clock a hundred times before, waiting for recess or the end of the day. Never anything this important. The class is paging through their books to memorize facts they'll forget in two weeks and all I can do is wait, wait, wait, wait, wait.

The next day it all comes down to this, and from my perfect vantage point in the utility closet, my shadow hasn't moved in a half hour and finally we've got about thirty seconds. My hair stands on end like the moment before a lightning strike. Time to move.

Mrs. Fury is so fat it takes her at least nine seconds to get up and walk to the doorway of the closet. I've tested this out a dozen different ways in the last month to get it just right. The boxes come off the shelves so easily and Mrs. Fury is probably muttering to herself, *Well my word. What on earth is going on back there this time?*

I'm watching, waiting for her to get up get up *get up get up* perfect. It wasn't going to hit anyone, the way I saw it; everyone was shocked and scared and crying, parents outraged, headline news; but no one got hurt. We were all too short, sitting in our desks, but she was tall enough.

It was just a couple senior high kids; they'd have gotten community service. It'd be all over every channel at five or six o'clock for a week, then they'd install a metal detector at the school next fall.

She's really moving today, not quite what I expected. Changing the future isn't as precise as seeing it. I have to slow her down just a bit so I leap out of the closet and convulse on the floor, fake an episode. She stops right in her tracks, the kids laughing while she mutters something along the lines of *My word, not again,* and then for a moment everything is perfect. It feels just like when you sense when you're on a tree branch that's about to break. You brace yourself and make the best of it, try to enjoy the rush of falling and hope it doesn't hurt too much when you land.

The kids all seated at their desks jump in unison as the window shatters and tiny bits of glass sparkle through the air. I savor the truly surprised look in her eyes. Then another burst of glass and Mrs. Fury's face turns from shock to panic to pain. Even with my ears ringing it's a beautiful sound.

The class is screaming and I can stop faking my episode now. No one is watching me. Mrs. Fury, she's the center of attention as her life splashes out Jackson Pollock style across the gold-star-of-achievement board.

And then she waits, stranded, dead on her feet for light years in that one flawless moment, hands grasping at nothing, a faint red puff still frozen in mid air, liquid arms reaching for mercy that will never come, all my classmates no more than statues. That day, my life got a little better and a whole lot worse.

4:

My cell phone buzzes in my pocket and I hit reject without even checking the display. Hate might be too strong a word in this case, but one person that really stretches my definition of the word "tolerate" is my half brother, Eddie. Picture a skinny seventeen-year-old wannabe high roller in a typical dingy, smoke-filled poker game, getting blitzed and hedging all he's got on a pair of fives. Last time something like this happened he lost his class ring. His birthday is in April so it had a little diamond chip in the center that he managed to convince some low life would be worth a fifty-dollar raise. This was no big deal to Eddie; he'd already dropped out.

How I came to nearly hate him, how he came to crash at my place, it all starts with Mona, with her love of coffee and my decision to work at Gallagher's and my inevitable interest in the world of gambling.

David heads out to Canterbury Park every weekend racing is in season, then during his weekly visits to the shop he chats it up with a couple regulars about his picks. He's the kind of guy who likes to sound successful at everything, talking about his house and garage in terms of square footage, his favorite trainers and jockeys in terms of their win-loss ratios and histories, invest- ments, other business ventures, the occasional real-estate deal.

I paid attention when he'd go on about his picks, tried to glean anything I could from him because if there's anything I've learned over the years, it's that you've got to notice when oppor- tunities come your way.

Later, I'd flip through the paper and see who won, and I found that David's betting strategy wasn't half bad. He generally picked a trainer or two who had the best records for the last twenty races or so. Whichever horses they were working with who came from good stock, those were the horses he bet on. It wasn't perfect, but it made sense, and he'd have you believe it made him a lot of money.

David had quite a few slick convertibles to back up that claim: A late nineties BMW M3, an Audi RX-8, a very recent Corvette, a bright yellow Honda 2000, a classic Porsche 911—and I mean, mid-sixties classic, before they all grew hips and sprouted those bulky spoilers. He even had one of those brand-new hundred-thousand-dollar Cadillac XLRs. The special edition convertible hardtop coupe he'd bragged about ordering for months, how it really cost a hundred-grand on the dot and only came in silver. As for me, driving around in what passes for an '89 Honda something or other (the badges were gone long before I acquired it) might have been a motivating factor in this scenario as well.

After a while I gave it a shot based on my gut instinct, which I've learned to trust. I'd circle some longshot horse or underrated trainer in the paper or write their names on a napkin and the next day I'd check my picks against the winners. I was doing a hundred-percent, which wasn't exactly a surprise so much as a nice development. The surprise was that cheap bets on these horses would pay handsomely thanks to their longshot status. This went on about six weeks before I got the guts to sneak in to Canterbury myself. I figured if I could get hold of a decent fake ID and keep a low profile I could make a little money, maybe buy a nice little red convertible for myself. Might as well enjoy life while I can. And who knows, maybe Mona would dig a guy with wheels. College girls like that kind of thing.

* * *

This morning, right after my break David pops out of his office for his weekly racing chat, gives the shop a quick once-over, then hands me a pile of fliers for his new gimmick; *"Open Mike Night"* which means I'll spend an hour or so printing off new fliers without the glaring typo. And the infuriating way he talks about all these ideas as if he's revolutionizing the food service industry. *Two-for-Tuesdays. The Soup and Sandwich Special. Caffeine Happy Hour.* But business is lagging, so whatever works.

After the printers, between making a couple cappuccinos and putting up fliers I get a bad feeling. I know right at that moment that I'll be at Canterbury Park that afternoon, but not on my own terms. My cell phone rings again.

Eddie.

Reject.

I can see it clearly. He's just gone all-in like some hotshot poker pro, bluffing with a low pair. His opponent's already paired the board with aces, so when the river card seals the deal, adding insult to injury with a third ace, he's done. This isn't even intuition, this is just the same old same old. Reluctantly, since I know this conversation is going to happen eventually, on the fourth or fifth call I answer.

"Hey, dude. It's Eddie."

As if I don't even have caller ID.

I say, "What's up, Lefty?"

"Shut up, ass hat."

"Look man, I'm at work, so b-be fast."

"You think we could meet sometime soon?"

"How much is it, Lefty?"

"Get off it, man. I'm in dying straights here."

"That's dire...never mind."

* * *

Lefty. Now that's a story few people know, so let me get it down on paper here once and for all in case I'm not around to tell it. The night of May 5, 2005—and I know because I have the ticket stub— I was at the Congress Theater in Chicago for Nine Inch Nails. I'd seen them before, closer to the Twin Cities, but this night was supposed to be special, something awful was going down. The dream had been so vague, so gritty and dark; I had no idea it would take me away from the concert. I had no idea it was Eddie.

Reeling in the throes of industrial rock, moving with the collective energy of thousands of rabid fans, not halfway through the set and I disappear completely, I mean gone, into a vision like I hadn't had in years. Was I awake? Yes. The man on stage, dressed in all black, flooded in pulsing lights, he was begging to the people, *Just how deep do you believe? Will you bite the hand that feeds?*

Then, silence, the pulse of the music in my chest fading as I fell into my own subconscious. Now here's a mind's-eye view of Eddie, screaming silent, earning his nickname as a couple thugs drag him towards an old meat grinder. At least then Eddie wised up, if only for a moment. He lied and said he was right-handed. Probably the smartest thing my brother had done in a long time. So they ground up his right hand instead of his left.

Coming back I could feel the backbeat pulsing deep in my chest while in silence I watched Eddie curled up in a ball on the floor and I made my way to the exit. My gut says, this is not just the future; it's the very near future. Eddie bleeds out just before sunrise, alone and cold, with a pair of bloodstained deuces left on his chest.

Then I'm back just in time to hear Trent Reznor pleading over the breakdown, *Are you brave enough to see? Do you want to change it?*

I take I-94 West toward the Twin Cities and about five hours later I find myself on the edge of South Saint Paul, parked, engine off, behind the boarded-up windows of an abandoned grocery store. Graffiti, broken bottles, a bag rustling against the fence. The dashboard clock glows 4:52 AM in LCD green and since I don't have the best relationship with time I wonder if I'm too late.

I find my way to the rear entrance, a door next to the loading dock, a rusty lock broken years ago. Moments later I'm creeping around the dilapidated meat section, shielding my face from the smell of years of slaughter soaked into the wood and concrete. Then there's the copper-penny tinge of fresh blood and suddenly here's Eddie, bleeding and unconscious at my feet. The sound of rats scurrying away, or maybe footsteps, I don't know. Without a word, I cinch up his homemade tourniquet and drag his unconscious body to the car. I drop him at the closest hospital and take off before first light, because the whole situation would have been way too difficult to explain.

"Yeah, I was in Chicago when I had this vision my brother was being mutilated by a bunch of cut-rate mobster goons so I drove to the exact spot where he was left for dead and then brought him here. What's so weird about that, officer?"

The next day I get the closest-living-relative phone call. I feign surprise and concern and make my way over, but Eddie is already rationalizing, trying to impress me with his quick thinking.

"'Cause really I'm left-handed, but they never knew."

He's proud of himself as he slurps room temperature cherry Jell-O through a straw.

"Those idiots ground up the wrong hand."

And it's not just that he can still sign his name. This way if he ever actually gets married, he can still wear a wedding ring.

"Yeah man...no idea how I got here, though. Someone just left me on the curb and took off. But hey, I can probably still play drums."

How is it that such blind optimism is wasted on guys like him? We used to fool around with the idea of starting a band, him on the drums and me on guitar.

"Think about it. The drummer from Def Leppard only has one arm."

"Well, Def Leppard were famous before their drummer lost his arm. Keep that in mind."

About a week later Eddie and I are in a little bar on Selby

Avenue in St. Paul where he's in good with the manager so there was no ID check necessary. Don't ask me how, but the little imp has a few worthwhile connections.

We were getting hammered and talking about life and love and loan sharks and avoiding this whole meat-grinder situation and well, I blame it on the alcohol. This was while his stump was still healing, right after getting out of the hospital. We gave up on pool, since I had an unfair advantage, got a table and ordered some beer.

"Coors Light? Are you kidding me?" He likes fancy, imported brews he can hardly pronounce.

"Hey, I have my reasons."

I read about this guy, Adolph Coors III, next in line to inherit the company, only he gets kidnapped for ransom. Should have only been a small speedbump on his way to having it made, but the kidnapper fouls it up and kills him in the process. The kidnapper, his name doesn't even matter, he goes to jail and the company passes on to someone else.

The part I identify with, the part that just kills me, is that poor, dead-as-a-doornail Adolph Coors III was allergic to beer in the first place. He'd spent his whole life looking forward to inheriting a company that produces a beverage he'd never be able to enjoy without going into anaphalactic shock, and even with all that on the table, fate or the universe or God or whatever didn't think it was enough and the man still ended up dead first. Call me a pessimist, but ever since I saw that documentary I've felt a bit of a kinship with the man. Of course, I hope I'm wrong. The thing that worries me is I'm usually not.

"Unbelievable. We're drinking for free and you order the beer-flavored water."

"Free beer is free beer. What do you care? It's not like Art over there is pouring us any free imports anyway."

After the first pitcher, he opens up about his financial situation, poker mostly, a little blackjack now and again. Like many in his position, he borrows a little, wins some, gets ahead for a few days, then loses it all. A few hundred bucks here and there, no big deal. He then borrows money from Dad to pay it off (who, out of guilt for being such a shitty father, glady wires the money), saying his car had broken down or gotten towed. Of course, father of the year doesn't really know Eddie's never even had his own car.

"But this time is different," he says, waving the foam #1 he's slid over his bandaged stump. "This time it's big."

He explains how, at sixteen, he's gotten in the red with three guys for about five grand each, at twenty-five percent. In a way I'm impressed. Not a lot of people his age could even pull off a gaff of that caliber.

Another pitcher of beer and I get a little too honest. I'm smart enough not to tell him it was me that dropped him off at the hospital, but I spill my guts about how I've been making a killing at the tracks. What can I say? He's sort of family.

I tell him how I'd made about fifteen grand over the last couple months with one little bet here or there. Bets that pay off twenty to one, fifty to one, sometimes more. I tell him I'm just good with the long shots. Instinct, I say. Then I really slip up when I tell him I'm a hundred-percent.

"We could be a team," he says. "We could put our money together."

"You don't have any money, remember?"

He'll be off work for at least a month from his collections job at the bank. The irony is completely lost on him there, sadly.

"Can't ask Dad for the money. Shit, I still don't know how I'm going to explain this," he says, wiggling the foam finger.

"We can burn that bridge when we get there. Let's figure this thing out first, okay."

The alcohol is talking, so I offer to take care of it right then and there, from my savings, but he turns me down. Says he's got a few bucks stashed in an old shoe in his apartment, saving up for a ring for his girlfriend. He offers to use that to get started at the tracks. His eyes well up with the sincerity of a struggling alcoholic at an AA meeting. Says he's turning over a new leaf.

"No more handouts, man." He glances at his hand, and I forgo the obvious one-liners that pile up one after another in my mind. "As long as you ain't shittin' me," he slurs. "So long as you're for real, about being a hundred percent, man, I say we do it."

If there's one thing worse than hearing counselors say "we" when they mean just you, it's my brother saying "we" when he means the both of us.

The next day, I hope maybe he'll be too hung-over to remember our conversation, but Art was good about cutting him off early since he drank for free and rarely tipped.

All of this, the stump and the beer and the honesty, it was about a year ago.

Now, today, in this actual moment of real, tangible time, I've got Eddie on the other end of the line hanging on my every word.

"Zeek. You there? Can we get together or not?"

"How much is it, Eddie?"

"Couple grand, maybe round it up to three. To get back on my feet, you know?"

"So you still have both your feet?"

"Real funny, asshole."

"Look, I've got some savings going again, so—"

"No, no, man. Just give me a long shot."

"Hey man, it's not like I can—"

"I know, I know, fine. But when you do pick them, they're golden."

"You got another fake?"

This would be his fourth.

"Yeah, and I grew a mustache, too. I seriously look about twenty-three or so. This isn't like the last one. There's no way I could have pulled off thirty-one for long. I figure this way I'm set."

"You got a new guy, or what?"

"That first dude was an amateur. This even has the iridescent bird logo thing, really convincing."

"Okay. I get off in another hour but I got some stuff to take care of right after. Meet me in Elliot Park around one?"

"No dice, man. That's too out in the open. How about Hell's Kitchen?"

A little themed diner on 10th street whose menu says "Damn good food" and I have to agree.

"Sure. Now is one o'clock okay?"

"Sure," he pauses. "You need a fake?"

"No, I'm set."

"I knew it. I knew you couldn't stay away, dude."

"I'm eighteen now, idiot."

I wait, but the penny never drops.

"So I'm old enough to use my own ID."

"Oh yeah, right. Okay, later."

"See you at one."

But he's already hung up.

I should let Eddie fend for himself. I'm not my half-brother's keeper. At the same time, I don't need his pathetic face around asking for money if I'm about to meet Mona any day now. No, getting him off my case, and fast, is a good idea.

5:

Outside it's the dead end of August and the sun's making a final stand. I grabbed an iced coffee before I left work. Now I set my guitar case down in the grass and take a sip, hold the cup against my face and let the condensation run down from my forehead. Okay.

I approach a table labeled "ORIENTATION STARTS HERE" in huge black letters on a neon-pink background. As I'm falling in behind other students, David thunders by in his old AC Cobra, the one his father passed on to him a couple years ago upon retirement.

"Now," David once told me, "Dad drives around southern Florida in a late fifties Buick ragtop. It suits a man in his golden years, you know?"

The Cobra, David said, has been kept in cherry condition from day one, his dad claims. Not a single restoration. Deep blue with white racing stripes, it's like watching a 700 hp cliché. David brags about having over a dozen four-wheel toys, but due to the rarity of original 427 Cobras, this is easily his most valuable. Half million, more if the market is right. He says there were only 55 made, so I guess I can see that.

David gives me a quick, manly salute of a wave as if to say, *You're on your own now.* The engine sends a rumbling shock wave through the hot, sticky air as he spins his tires around the corner and speeds off toward the highway. The smell of burnt rubber wafts by and as the smoke clears I may as well be alone.

* * *

A screaming pink orientation sign reflects across the faces of anyone within ten feet, luring me past the point of no return. A somewhat portly guy with a laminated nametag slung around

35

his neck proclaiming "Hi, my name is JOSHUA" walks up to meet me halfway. Summer-camp counselor's smile, only one of the dozens of happy people running around in khaki shorts and bright pink t-shirts with the letters SAC on them; pink seems to be the theme this year.

"Hey, nice headphones. So what brings you to Asbury Bible College?"

My throat closes in on itself as if my stomach dropping pulled some sort of drawstring. Everything inside me is clinched at the B-word word. Oh Mona, what have you gotten me into?

"B-bible college?" My words hang in the air.

The only reason I decided to enroll here is because in my dreams, sometimes Mona is sitting by a tree reading, and behind her I could see the word 'Asbury' but tree limbs obscured the rest.

JOSHUA redirects. "I'm sorry, Asbury 'University'," he makes little air quotes, "technically speaking. We've had university status since ninety-nine, so we're accredited now, but we're still in the good old AG system."

I hand him some registration forms and I'm sure my face says, *What the Hell is the AG system?*

He flips through a couple forms, "Hey, alright. Says here...yep, I thought you looked like a musician."

My fingers tighten around the handle of my guitar case; it's all I can do to keep from being sarcastic.

JOSHUA pats me on the back and says, "I play too. We should totally jam some time."

"Sounds great."

"And you know...Ezekiel is a good name."

"That so?"

"Absolutely, man. It means 'Strength of God'."

He slaps a sticker on my chest with my name in all caps just like his, in case someone needs to read it at a distance of eighty yards.

"Let me show you around."

"So this will be a guided tour?" Please say no.

"Absolutely, man. We want you to feel right at home." The way he says "we", that smile on his face; we're already best friends. "Now what dorm are we in?"

"Actually, I live up the road here."

"An apartment?" His face twists ever so slightly.

"Yeah."

"Off campus?" Twists a little more, with rays of jealousy peeking through.

"Well, yeah."

"How'd...you manage that?"

"I'm not a full-time student, so it'll be easier to pay as I go. The dorms cost a lot more than rent, for a basement apartment at least."

I'd soon learn that having your own apartment here is like having your own car in high school, a luxury I never enjoyed. As the tour convenes, JOSHUA remarks that most people in the neighborhood have no idea the college even exists, let alone the fact that it's a Bible college, so I don't feel quite so stupid for having missed the Bible-college angle myself. I've worked at the coffee shop a hundred yards away and never had a clue that one of those buildings was a chapel.

"We'll get you plugged in to a guy's floor so you can get involved in different activities and small groups, prayer circles, discipleship, stuff like that. And every guy floor is paired up with a sister floor. We'd hate for you to feel all alone in a big city like this."

I don't bother mentioning that I've lived in Minneapolis my whole life; instead I suddenly wonder how much counseling JOSHUA here must have been through. All those "we" phrases, that pasted-on smile. If he hasn't been through years of counseling then he's studying psychology or something.

He flips through some pages on his clipboard and says, "Okay, next stop is the library, 'cause I guess we don't need to go to financial aid, huh?"

The huge white building looms ahead of us, its six-columned facade like a set of twenty-foot teeth ready to devour me whole.

"You think we could skip the library?" Knowing your days are numbered and that your last one will take place in a room full of books tends to make you a little cautious.

"Allergic to studying, eh?"

"Oh, you know how it is..." I trail off, hoping he won't push it. He searches my face for a reaction he can read, but unlike Eddie my poker face is like a stone.

"Okay..." He shrugs and flips to the next page on his clipboard. "We'll head to the gym next."

"What's in the gym?"

"All kinds of fun stuff. Don't think I'm going to spoil the surprise."

As if "all kinds of fun stuff" is going to come as more of a shock than the fact that I've unwittingly registered to attend Bible college. Every piece of paper I'd filled out to register, every class schedule I'd glossed over in search of the music classes; how did I miss it? All those pages had the word 'University', but apparently that was a mere 'air quotes' technicality.

Oh Mona. Are you studying to be a missionary? Or a nun? What on earth are we going to have in common?

I see us meeting for coffee, then she starts talking about Jesus and I begin to cringe and somehow all these years I've missed this side of her and now I'm all wrong. I'm faithless and she's not going to want anything to do with me.

There we are, sipping coffee in my death scene when she confesses that what she really wants in life is to preach to a little, newly discovered tribal colony of some third-world jungle. Then I tell her I'm not so sure about God, how I'm still working that one out, which is why all these years, night after night, she panics and then everything fades to white and I wake up feeling a few hours closer to dead.

But I don't have time to reassess this final dream in light of these new developments. JOSHUA pushes through the gymnasium doors and we're greeted by the pulsing thump of up-tempo techno Jesus music and a wave of ice-cold AC. I suppose the air was nice. Inside a dozen booths in the same bright pink theme with bamboo poles and tiki torches host various student activities. JOSHUA hands me off to a girl named BETHANY, who says, "Let's get you a lay."

BETHANY reads my face and giggles at the double meaning.

"A flower necklace, silly, as in: L-E-I. It's a Hawaiian theme. I'm with SAC, which is the Student Activities Committee," she points to each letter on her shirt. I try not to stare, but the air conditioning is doing wonders underneath. She whips out a flower necklace and holds it out. I lean forward, get lei'd, and then she shows me all the fun ways to be involved on campus.

We eventually get to the booth for the music department to see about the jazz ensemble while BETHANY skips over to lei the next newbie. JOSHUA must have been responsible for making all the nametags; a guy named GREG tells me about the different jazz ensembles and how the auditions would work. He asks me if I like hymns. "…Because a lot of times, we take an old standard and really jazz it up. You wouldn't even recognize the chord structure, but the melody is there to point you right back to 'Amazing Grace' or 'The Old Rugged Cross'. 'Washed in the Blood'."

I consider making a 'Raining Blood' reference, easily Slayer's all time best song, but I think better of it. I talk with GREG for a few minutes and decide it can't be all that bad, so I sign up for the latest audition slot available this afternoon, in case it takes a while with Eddie out at Canterbury. Done with that, I'm making a beeline for the door when JOSHUA intercepts me.

"Hey, buddy, where are we off to now? There's a raffle in another twenty minutes, but you gotta be here to win."

"I need to get going."

"Now where on earth could you—"

"Hell's Kitchen."

JOSHUA looks somewhat bewildered, as if the word itself holds some sort of power. But right then if there is somebody upstairs, he smiles on me – my cell phone rings. I make that faux polite, 'I've got to take this call' gesture and push on through the doors past him.

Out in the heat again I say, "Buddy, am I glad to hear from you."

Nothing.

"Hello?" I ask, irritated, not wanting to deal with any more of Eddie's shit, but it's not Eddie.

On the other end, a man clears his throat and with a very controlled voice he asks, "Is this Ezekiel?"

"Is this a sales call?"

I'm ready to hang up when the voice says something so quiet it sounds like static at first.

"I just want to say...thank you."

The voice is quiet but not small, and the controlled intensity makes the tiny hairs on my neck try to stand up through the sweat.

"I'm sorry, did you say, 'Thank you'?"

Nothing.

"Who is this?"

"You were dead on."

"What the f—"

"No need to worry about that now. We'll see you soon."

click

Okay, this guy knows me, but his voice, it's older. A teacher? Or maybe he smokes. I close my eyes and wait...nothing. He's off the radar. The possibilities begin to whiz around my head.

I can see some weirdo stalker in tall leather boots rubbing bright red lipstick on his face and clean-shaven chest, laid out on a futon amidst a cloud of incense smoke, circling my name on a list of people from high school he's decided to kill. It could be any number of guys I'd hounded to keep myself away from the bottom of the pecking order.

Around seventh grade my stutter had become a thing of the past, but with all those early episodes, the memory remained. I had to turn the tables, so I picked out a few social weaklings to flat-out torture. It was the only move available to a guy like me.

And I don't expect you to like me because of this, but try and understand where I'm coming from. I simply went from prey to predator. People do it every day.

Still, as hard as I try, I can't imagine anyone that would have the nerve to get back in touch. And to say "Thank you" doesn't add up at all.

This time I check the caller ID before answering. It says Eddie, but even so I'm nervous.

"Hello?"

"Where the Hell are you?"

"God, it's good to hear your voice."

"What? Really?"

He's as surprised to hear it as I am to say it.

"Yeah, never mind. What's up?"

"Dude, it's after one. Where are you?"

Eddie's on time and I'm late? It's a good day for long shots.

"Give me five minutes."

"Fuckin' A, man."

click

At that I find a trashcan and toss my flower necklace inside, and I don't just drop it in, no, I break the string and rip the flowers off in a feeble attempt to take control of the moment, to shake off the unease, as if the lei has anything to do with it.

6:

So Eddie. His wardrobe is an amalgam of polyester shirts with Japanese characters or tribal designs or flaming aces coming out of the chest pocket, clever shit like that. He's always got a pair of silver-tinted sunglasses resting on top of spikey hair going one way or another, with a big silver chain around his tiny neck; links so thick you'd think they would hurt.

I usually bite my tongue.

"You know, you really stand out in a crowd."

"What?"

"This whole getup. It screams for attention."

"This is my image, man."

"For a guy who's trying to lay low..." I take a final sip and drop the cup in the backseat.

"You were saying?"

"You blend in like a nudist in Alaska."

"Har har."

I try telling him I work better alone, but he swears up and down he won't make the same mistakes he made last time. I tell him he has a knack for making all new mistakes and he slugs me with his bony stump.

Rubbing my arm I say, "Maybe drive around for a while. You could go grab us a case of beer, for the celebration later. See if your fake is as good as you say."

"Look, don't worry, it's cool. Here." He digs it out of the front pocket of his jeans. We're stopped at a light and a little old lady pulls up next to us in a giant white Oldsmobile. She has a curly white wig and those huge sunglasses that go over prescription glasses. Just as Eddie's hips are heaving up and down, in and out of view, she glances over. With his hands groping around in his pocket, well, the old lady's jaw drops open, hand to her mouth, and she takes a hasty right.

I hold back a laugh and say, "First thing's first, put that in your wallet. No one carries their ID in the front pocket." He does so. "Now, take out your old stuff and leave it all in the glove box so there's no confusion."

"Just check it out first, okay."

It's not half bad and the mustache does make him look a bit older. A honk tells me the light must have turned green. I hand the ID back and hit the gas.

He doesn't give up trying to convince me to take him along. He tries reasoning and arguing and whining and eventually resorts to a good old-fashioned guilt trip. Something about needing a second chance and how no one has ever believed in him. Not Dad, not Joanne, no one.

"She was always nicer to you, man."

"There were other factors involved."

"Yeah, well, she was my real mom."

I throw him a pissed-off look and he backs off from that angle, but regardless of my reasoning he stands his ground the rest of the drive until we pull into the lot. I was about ready to cave in when he has a sudden change of heart.

I pull out one of Dad's old blue tags and aim for the handicapped space saying, "You want to act like a gimp when we get out, or is it up to me?"

Then Eddie slumps down into his seat and says, "Keep driving."

I follow his line of sight before his eyes dart away. A couple gorillas dressed like twin nightclub owners, Eddie's kind of people, are scanning the lot, standing by a pile of cigarette butts near the casino entrance.

"Friends of yours?" I back out of the spot.

"Maybe I've seen them around once or twice."

"Yeah? How's your stump feeling?"

"Just head around the side there, fuck nuts."

"Look, first post is in about ten minutes so I don't have time to screw around. Are those the guys you owe or not?"

"No, they're just thugs, but they talk too much."

"Who cares if they talk too much."

"And they know people I'd rather not hear about me right now. I'll get the beer, okay. Just get out over there in the back, next to the little Mazda."

I have a gut feeling to say no, to find another spot, but then I get a more urgent feeling to put some distance between Eddie and me. My second impulse wins, so I park next to the lone car.

"Look, man, help me out a little, okay. I'm out here saving your skin. Again. So keep a low profile for right now." I put it in park, leave the engine running and get out.

"Well, for starters, you could take off that name tag, short bus."

"Shit." I crumple it and toss it into the backseat. "Try not to lose your license again, okay."

"Don't worry," he says as he slides across the seats, "I don't have a license to lose. Well, not a real one, anyway."

My stomach sinks a little as he lurches away in my sad excuse of a car and then the chirp of a car alarm startles me. I can't seem to find the resolve to turn around.

* * *

"Zeek, is that you?"

I knew I recognized that Mazda.

"Hey, D-David, how you been? I see you've dropped off the Cobra."

"It's being detailed for the car show next weekend, so I thought I'd take this one out for the rest of the day." He rubs his chin like he's having a really deep thought. "You know, they say the way a man treats his car is the way he lives his life."

This coming from the guy who owns so many little sports cars. I consider a split-personality joke, but self-deprecating humor is always best with your superiors.

"Well don't worry, I b-bathe more than my car."

He laughs. "That's good to hear, but that's not what I mean." He shoves his thumb at his chest and leans in, drops his voice like he's sharing some kind of secret. "I never let anyone else drive. I'm in charge, you know? It's an ancient Chinese proverb."

"The ancient Chinese had proverbs about cars?"

"Well...no. I mean it's based on ancient Chinese wisdom...and stuff." His demeanor shifts. "Aren't you a little young?"

He's smiling but I can't get a good read, so I scramble.

"Oh, I'm uh, meeting some friends and..."

"You know, I thought I saw you around a couple times last summer. Don't worry about it. I did the same thing when I was a kid. Boy, I loved the slots back then."

"Well, you got me." Wake up, idiot. "Actually I turned eighteen in July." God dammit, what good is seeing the future if I can't remember right now?

"Oh, that's right. Well, good luck." His little yellow convertible chirps again as he walks off.

"Yeah, you too."

* * *

I did pretty well that afternoon. I got a couple good feelings here and there, but I really cleaned up thanks to a horse named *Vegas Excalibur*. One look at that name, it shot through me like a lightning bolt and his odds were the worst I'd seen in a long time.

I put twenty down on *Vegas Excalibur* with *Other People's Money* coming in second, another decent underdog, and *Little Wonder* to round out the trifecta. That one bet alone paid off a little over twenty-three hundred dollars. I had to resist the urge to put more down, the chance it might throw off the odds or invite more bets.

I'd walked in with fifty bucks of Eddie's money, still saving for that engagement ring, plus twenty-five of my own, but I walked out with just shy of four grand.

On our way home, I told him I hadn't done too bad and that I only lost two bets, 'cause I simply can't have him putting that much faith in me. He settles for twenty-five hundred, saying that will make his bookie happy and cover food for the next couple weeks, and I keep about fourteen hundred for myself.

I drop him off at his place, he insists I drive around the side near the alley, then he runs around like an idiot ninja, dashing between parked cars and knocking over a couple trashcans on his way to the back entrance. It's like watching a real-life cartoon. I'd hope for an anvil to drop on his head and make my life easier, but I'd have definitely seen that coming.

Driving home I can finally breathe a little. I've got cash in my pocket and my brother should be off my case for at least another month. There are much bigger things to worry about. Tomorrow is my big day.

7:

Home. Rifling through a stack of papers until I find the student handbook that came with my registration packet. I pull the light on and there it is, right below the huge Asbury University logo, in eight- or nine-point Arial lettering:

- An Accredited Bible College -

It's not exactly fine print, but it wasn't obvious either. So what else did I miss? I fumble with three different remotes, crank up the stereo then thumb through the handbook. I find the spot that says if you're a full-time student you have to live on campus. I guess I caught that last time, which is why I took ten credits instead of twelve. Why pay for a dorm? I already have a place. What I hadn't read is that full-time students are also required to attend chapel five days a week, right before lunch. Now there's a bullet I'm happy to dodge.

And apparently AG stands for Assemblies of God, which sounds vaguely familiar. Way back in grade school my Dad would take us to this church with a logo that looked like a burning dove dive-bombing the planter around the sign. Dad was an usher and I remember hearing people talk about things being approved by the AG or not, but I never thought about it much. I was a kid and that was grownup stuff. Now I know.

Asbury also has a behavior agreement I was supposed to sign and date and hand in with my registration. Mine's still attached: page xxiii in the front. Apparently they don't allow gambling, so I'll have to keep my side job under wraps. Then again, if God's watching, then I'm sure he understands. It's not like the Student Activities Committee isn't selling raffle tickets all week. I'm sure they'd excuse a little horse racing in light of that.

Page after page of Bible-related classes spread out before me, things I'd skimmed over when all I was interested in were English, Math, Music.

I must have been on autopilot the day I filled out my registration forms 'cause how on earth did I miss all this? This isn't like missing a stop sign hidden behind a shrub, having a near miss with an old lady on a scooter. This is like running your car directly into a building at ninety miles an hour and blaming it on lack of coffee. Speaking of, I head to the kitchen for a warm up, and that seems to help bridge the mental gap. What choice do I have? For better or worse I'm in. I have to survive the Asbury Bible College Community, to last long enough to meet Mona. Nothing else matters.

I've nearly read the handbook cover to cover when the changer switches CDs from Nine Inch Nails to Wes Montgomery, quite a stylistic jolt that serves to remind me about jazz auditions. The clock says it's a few minutes after five, which makes me late. I grab my MP3 player, backpack and guitar and hustle toward campus to find a huge crowd gathered between the non-descript chapel and the main building, blocking the entire street. I detour around back.

The pink Hawaiian-themed schedule of events says to go to room 204, but when I get there the room is empty. Not only that, but there isn't a person in sight. Even the halls are silent.

Killing the MP3 player just as Kerry King starts shredding the breakdown on Skeleton Christ, I step inside. Along the back of the room are stacks of chairs, a baby grand at the far side of the room, a couple small amps next to a jazz-style drum kit; some chord changes are scrawled on the grease board. Footfalls in the hallway sound promising. I lean out for a look, don't recognize the face but he's still wearing a nametag so I risk it.

"GEOFF?" He looks up and smiles without over doing it. Good sign. "Out of curiosity, d-do you know anything about the jazz auditions?"

"Naw man, sorry. Pastoral major." He forces these words through a surprisingly thick drawl. "This yer first year?" I notice he's wearing blue-tinted glasses, an odd addition to his crew cut and business-casual attire. His look says middle management but his accent and that crooked smile, those blue-tinted shades; pure Trailer-Parks-Ville, Alabama.

"First year, yeah."

"Lemme guess, music major?"

"You got it."

"Sweet, man. Hey, you gonna make the ice-cream social?" He thumbs toward the horde of people outside, the crowd I made an effort to avoid moments before.

"Oh, that's what that is?"

"Yeah, man. You should check it out. Gets better every year."

"Well, I'm supposed to audition..."

"Okay, son. But I wanna see you there later. They got kegs."

And I'm sure my face said, *Kegs? Really?*

"Root beer, man. Best floats this side of the Missippi," he says, completely dropping the middle of the word. "See you there."

He waits, smiling, so I say, "You bet."

Blue Glasses GEOFF starts to whistle as he makes his way toward the stairs at the other end of the skyway. It's about the moment I realize he's whistling the Andy Griffith Show theme that I look up and here comes JOSHUA from the other direction, though I almost don't recognize him without the pink shirt and emboldened nametag. Instead he's wearing faded jeans and a dark tee shirt. He sees me sitting there, all alone, gives me his best-friend smile and looks down at his guitar case.

"Hey, man, I told you we should get together and jam. How'd your audition go?"

"No one was here."

"That's Greg for you. Don't worry about it. There's always another set of auditions in a week or so."

"Good to know."

At that he plops down and pulls out an impressive acoustic-electric guitar: it's beautiful, understated, made with top-notch wood and the soundhole is off-center, shaped like a tear drop.

"What, uh...what do you have there?" I ask, trying not to sound too interested.

"It's a McPherson. This kid that goes to school here, his dad makes them. They're really incredible. All hand made and every-thing."

"Well, if it sounds half as good as it looks, I'll be impressed. So we've got the same major, then?"

"No, not in the music program. This is my fourth year, pastoral major, so I only have time to get into little jam sessions now and then. Doing an open mic later, so I figured I'd just bring it along and now here we are."

"Ah..." I'm scrambling for an exit but I come up blank.

"So why don't you pull that bad boy out of its case and show me what you've got?"

I consider telling him I'm on my way to the ice-cream social, but the phrase dies in my mouth. What can I do? I flip the locks, unprepared to hold my beater up to his veritable work of art. I give it a couple strums, tune up the top two strings and he's already starting to work through the chords on the board.

It's almost a relief when a handful of guys and a blonde girl, all wearing shades of black and gray, come into the room and start unloading a series of hard plastic flight cases. JOSHUA begins to pack up his guitar without a word so I get the hint and I'm ready to follow him out the moment he's done.

About ten seconds later a short man with beady eyes and a receding hairline comes in. He's in a three-piece black on black on black suit. As JOSHUA snaps the last clasp on his case, the short man clears his throat.

"Boys," he says, "we've got this room from five-thirty on, so we're going to need you to clear out in the next couple minutes. Thanks." He never bothers to look at us.

JOSHUA leads the way and when we're out of earshot he explains how I'll be seeing a lot of this guy around.

"That was Barry Loch, head of the music department. And all

those little clones of his, that was 'Worship Live!' complete with a little exclamation point at the end. They do the music for chapel and stuff."

We push through the doors to go outside and are immediately surrounded by a throng of hyperactive Hawaiian shirts. I look over to a table with four kegs and Blue Glasses GEOFF is manning one labeled DIET and waving emphatically. I keep my eyes moving.

A scrappy-looking guy grabs JOSHUA by the arm. "Hey, let's go check out that open mic. It's right up the block here."

"Sure, I'm in." Then he nods to me. "By the way, this is Ezekiel. And Ezekiel, this is Josh."

The scrappy guy nods, "Number two."

"So," looking to JOSHUA, "you're number...?"

"One. Yep, I'm the original."

"So where's Josh number three?" I thought I was being clever, but Number Two puts his head down and lowers his voice.

"He died in a car accident last summer." After that, they both look to the sky and genuflect.

"Oh shit."

Number Two says, "Kidding. He's working right now. Cool guy, actually."

Number One says, "Yeah, he's our music store hook-up. If you need anything, he gets forty percent off at The Wood Shed."

"On University?"

Number Two says, "That's the one. He's the guy with the ring of fire tattooed around his neck."

"Seriously?"

"Yeah."

"That guy?"

They nod, practically giggling at my doubt.

"The one with a dozen piercings and over four thousand dollars' worth of ink?"

"Oh, you know him?"

"Yeah, he's a metal genius. You mean to tell me—"

Number Two says, "Yeah, his name is Joshua, too. What's so weird about that?"

I was thinking, he's a fucking Bible thumper?

"So now you know Number One, Two and Three at least."

"Wait, how many are there?"

"Who knows?" JOSHUA says, feigning seriousness again. "Probably dozens. It seems back in the early- to mid-eighties, ours was a very popular name. There are six on my floor alone, which is why we resorted to the numbering system. These Swedish last names are too hard to say and usually lend themselves to dirty nicknames, so numbers are a pretty safe route."

"I can see that."

"Anyway, I go by Joshua, because going by 'Number One' sounds pretentious."

"And I'm Josh, without the 'U-A', 'cause going by 'Number Two' sounds like, well, you know."

"Shit."

"Well, I would have said, pooh, but there you have it. Shit."

JOSHUA says, "So numbers three on up go by their rank, so to speak."

"So what happens when you graduate?"

Josh says, "Huh. I don't know."

JOSHUA says, "Never thought about it. Anyway, you want to come with us, or are you holding that guitar to make yourself look cool for the ladies?"

"I hate to bail, but I think I'm gonna go grab some coffee. I've been up since five."

Josh says, "Then you should definitely come. It's over at this little coffee shop. Geronimo's or..." He points up the street and it dawns on me that he means Gallagher's. I desperately need the caffeine so I say, "Count me in."

The three of us make our way down the street, our long

shadows slinking up the sidewalk as the noise of the ice-cream social fades into the background. We pass Elliot Park while half a dozen pink shirts are breaking down tables and hauling them toward the school.

The shop is teeming with life and Lissa's head bobs in the background just under the menu. I catch her attention and her eyes say, *Get the Hell back here*. We only schedule one person from three till close because it's usually slow, but I would soon learn that David has dropped off quite a few buy-one-get-one-free cards to be handed out during Asbury's orientation. Probably too many.

It was down to making frozen lattes for a crowd of fifty college students with Barbie Manson at the register or having a jam session with these dudes. Coffee seemed the lesser of two evils where there'd at least be the prospect of a few tips. The Joshes head into the community room where the open-mic gear is set up and when the door closes behind them I feel a touch of hope. Maybe I can slip out once the line dies down.

Lissa hands me a list of drinks she's still working on and neither of us speak any more than absolutely necessary until we're basically done, which takes a solid forty-five minutes.

"Look, I've got a concert tonight. Cover for me until Sarah gets here." Her face says, *Don't you dare try and get out of this*.

I'm not fazed.

"I can't, but Sarah could probably come in early. She's been wanting more hours anyway."

She stares, one eye closes halfway. "Whatever. Call her while I count the tips."

That doesn't take long. For all our trouble we split a lousy seven-fifty, which elicits a long string of swear words from Lissa, which, in turn, hastens a few rather naïve-looking girls out the door. Lissa takes off the moment Sarah walks in the door so I explain the situation with the drink vouchers and tell her to call if there's another rush.

On my way out, a couple licks of John Coltrane's Giant Steps catches my attention and my gut says I have to check it out. To my amazement, Number One isn't just some kid with a flashy guitar. He's soloing with hummingbird speed while Number Two hammers out the fast-paced chord changes. I stand in awe while the two of them play through the whole tune and then seamlessly gear down into a medium tempo, bluesy version of 'Summertime'.

Part of me wants to stay and listen, but a bigger part of me is just plain exhausted. I lurch home and fall face first onto my couch. Sleep.

8:

Mona.

The glass ceiling approaches, indifferent and unrelenting, a silent image of things to come and all I can do is watch, read lips, and she's saying, "You know, I thought you were a Catholic, back then, at the coffee shop. The crucifix, the long hair. I totally wrote you off."

I gaze into the inevitable.

"Yeah, not that it matters, I guess. You've been playing much better."

"Doesn't mean I ever win."

"You're still learning."

No, I've been practicing for years.

"Well, you've definitely broken my stereotype of a long-haired, guitar-playing coffee-shop guy."

"Good to know."

"So, what is it that makes you, you know..."

Her delicacy seems deeper than mere political correctness. It's in her eyes, a real sense of empathy. No "we" statements, none of that faux intimacy bullshit.

"Stutter? Why d-do I s-s-stutter?"

"Forget it. I'm sorry."

"It's f-f-fi-fin—" Dammit. "It's okay."

"I'm sorry I asked, I didn't mean to bring anything up."

"Third g-grade. It s-started in the third grade. I went through a lot that year."

She nods to go on.

"B-but this stutter, it started when m-m-my t-teacher died."

Her face changes and she looks right into me and something changes in her eyes, like she's waiting for me to take it back.

"What is it?"

"No, nothing." Obviously flustered, but for some reason

trying to spare me the details of her own story for the sake of learning mine. "Did you really like your teacher?"

Oh Mona, I can't tell you that.

"D-Did I like her?"

"I guess most kids that age—"

"I hated her." Get it all out. "In fact, I k-killed her."

"What?"

"My teacher. It w-w-was me."

She shakes her head.

"I k-killed my teacher."

I lose focus and my mind races. *Don't you want to know more? To know why? Or how?*

Everything slows down and she turns her head, left and right at the same time, slow-motion disbelief, then almost motionless and fading to white as a bright blur consumes my vision. The image loses rationality. The room we're in, the room we will be in, loses all sense of definition. Books fly from the shelves and glass glitters through the air like wind-driven snow broken only by a dissonant electronic pulsing sound that cuts through the entirety of the dream world and sends me hurtling back to the present.

* * *

Reaching, feeling, probing. Fingers racing along waves of cloth and skin, across warm and cold, sensing stillness then vibration and I turn off the alarm clock.

Sound means it's now, it's okay, I can breathe.

Five-fifteen in the AM, Sunday morning, an unknown but small amount of time between me and zero. Shake off the exhaustion; rub the sleep from my eyes. Autopilot.

I slip into a pair of mostly clean jeans and a Blue Man Group concert shirt without thought. Coffee maker, piss, brush teeth, look at hair, shrug, put on a hat. Pour coffee. Give that a minute to settle in. Keys, wallet, headphones. Out the door and off to work.

And then a surge of adrenaline shoots through my mind and down toward my stomach, like that sickly excited feeling at the top of a roller coaster when you start to accelerate but you still can't see the bottom.

Today is the day. I have to look better than this. I rush back inside and throw on a pair of khakis and a slightly nicer t-shirt, one of the few I own without some band logo or musical reference, and I rush back out into the chill of an autumn sunrise. The cool morning air helps the waking process. A couple shots of espresso should do the rest.

9:

Honestly, I don't hate Jim. I interviewed him a couple weeks ago, and he's a pretty nice guy from a small town on the border of Minnesota and Iowa. However, he didn't make a great first impression.

"Name's Jim, but ya'll can call me Jim-Bo."

Lissa and I both laughed. I had the idea he was poking fun at himself. I'm sure Lissa was just being mean. Jim-Bo, however, was dead serious when he asked what was so funny. Knowing Lissa was likely to be a jerk, I stepped in.

"Well, Jim-Bo is longer than your real name."

"Yeah...?"

"I thought the purpose of having a nickname was so it would be shorter. Like, we call Allison here Lissa. People call me Zeek instead of Ezekiel. With Jim-Bo, it's...longer." I leave out how stereotypically redneck it sounds.

Ever since he started he's shown interest in the coffee roaster so I've been showing him how it works. If nothing else it keeps him away from Lissa.

"Every batch is different. You have to learn all the steps by the book, then you have to throw the book out the window and, d-ah...do it by feel."

"Feel?"

Jim can hardly hear me over the shop-vac. Hell, I can hardly hear me.

"That's right." I yell, even though we're almost face-to-face.

"Feel, smell, looks – all those things are important. This machine is actually warming up until after the first couple batches, so anything you roast after that will be more predictable, but those first couple you really have to watch."

"So what are you doing now?"

"The first step in roasting is actually cleaning the machine from yesterday's roast. A couple hours of roasting will leave a few pounds of this husk-like stuff in the machine, from the beans. This is the only way to clean it out, but if you open this main access plate right after roasting you'll burn your face off. Takes a couple hours to cool, so we d- ah...we do it first thing in the morning the next day."

I click the shop-vac off and screw the access plate back in to place. This is Jim's first opening shift, so he'll finally get to see the entire process.

Then my heart stops. She's leaning against her tree like I've seen a thousand times before, reading in the early morning light, the brisk fall air rustling around her, only this time it's real. Close enough to make eye contact.

"Aren't you getting hot?"

"What?"

"The roaster. Don't you get hot standing here all that time?"

"Well, you roast at four hundred degrees so yeah, it gets pretty hot. But I like the heat."

"Me too. I'd like to head south some day. Get away from this frozen tundra, yup."

"Right there with you."

"Get a farm, maybe some cows. Grow corn."

"Well..."

There's a persistent knock on the door.

"Look who's locked out." I smile.

"Why do you lock the door if we're in here?"

"This is the city, man. Last summer there was a girl getting things ready to open and she got robbed. Thirty seconds, it was over. Now we always staff at least two people in the mornings and we lock the door until we're ready to open, just in case."

"Wow."

"I'm a little tangled up here with the shop-vac," my leg's wrapped up in the cord. "You think you could..." I point to the door.

"Sure." He lumbers over.

Instead of bouncing around, Lissa lurches inside with one hand to her head and the other palm out toward us, Don't-Even-Ask style. She drops her jacket on the floor next to the coat rack, her two-sizes-too-small baby doll looking ready to burst. Behind the counter she takes three notebooks out of her backpack and plops them down next to the cash register.

"Look, don't bitch, okay. I lost my keys at the concert last night."

"Well, Jim's ready for your words of wisdom."

"Why don't you hang out with Jim-Bo and teach him about roasting some more. I work better alone on days like this."

They were mostly days like this for her, but I keep my mouth shut. Jim was lost behind his mop of somewhat wavy dishwater-blond hair, a one-man campaign against hygiene, which is mostly why Lissa already hates working with him. What Lissa makes up for in looks she lacks in personality, and she looks nearly perfect.

"Lissa, that extra fifty cents an hour for being the trainer means you actually have to train people at some point." She's been putting it off for over a week.

"Whatever, I'll show him tomorrow. I've got a crazy headache right now and a huge test this afternoon, so please." She throws a half-dozen muffins into the case.

"Don't classes start next week? I mean... it's Sunday."

"Not for summer school, Jim-Bo. It's a make-up test, okay? At the U, the real big school across the river with a football team and everything. And by the way," she turns to me, "why doesn't Jim-Bo here have to work Friday or Saturday, like, ever?"

"I help on the farm on weekends."

"I wasn't asking you."

"Okay, you guys. Come on."

"Whatever. Look, Zeek, you think you can roast a little later, after I'm gone? That thing is so fucking loud and I really can't take it right now."

"How late d-do you work?"

"Nine, but you can let me leave when Shelley gets here."

Oh yeah. I'm the assistant manager, an extra twenty-five cents an hour (don't ask me how that math works), which basically means I get to make almost no decisions and do more work. Lissa has it in good with David so she calls her own shots most of the time.

"And what's with the khakis, roaster boy?"

I shrug. "So what about Jim? You gonna train him or not?" He's got his head down as if he's used to being in this position, people talking about him like he's not there.

"Look, Shelley gets here at 6:30, so why don't you guys go, I don't know, do guy stuff until then? When she gets here I'll take off and you can do whatever the Hell you want."

To Jim I say, "Come on. We need to put out the tables and chairs anyway."

"You lock the chairs up at night, too?"

"People will take anything given the chance."

Lissa tosses me the keys to unlock the furniture and Jim follows. Outside, I can't help but stare. She's right there leaning against that tree, her tree. Our tree soon enough.

* * *

The sunrise explodes, reflecting back from the thousand windows of the Minneapolis skyline to the west. It takes a lot of effort to keep my gaze fixed on Mona for that long moment with the skyline's glare in my face, but it's worth it. She's real, and she's really there. What difference could a few sunspots make?

I put out a couple chairs and we sit. Keeping track of Mona in my periphery, I tell Jim about getting the machine up to temperature, slowly, then dropping the beans into the drum and bringing the batch up to about four hundred fifty degrees over a period of five minutes.

"Which feels longer than you think when you're standing there staring at your watch. Then you let the beans roast at that temperature until they start to crack. Once they begin to crack steadily, like popcorn, bring the roast down to four-oh-five. Quickly. The first crack means the core temperature of the actual beans has reached about four hundred, which is really the key for producing the complex carbon chains that give each bean its character."

Jim's attention is locked onto me like his life depends on learning to roast coffee. Mona is engrossed in her book and I wonder what she's reading. Is it something I should have read? Could I ever really see the book? I can't remember. Maybe it's poetry and I wouldn't get it anyway, or maybe it's something cool like *Fight Club* or *The Catcher in the Rye*. Or maybe it's a Bible and she's memorizing scripture for some kind of street preaching gig this weekend. God, I hope not.

"Zeek?"

"Right. So then you hold the temperature at around four-oh-five until the second crack. After that, the next few things you d-ah...the next few steps will determine the type of roast." I keep forgetting to avoid those plosive d-words. The worst.

Mona turns the page.

"If you want a Full City roast, which has a lighter flavor, then d-drop them into the cooling tray the moment you hear the second crack and you're d- ah... then you're finished."

Fuck. Hold it together.

"This will preserve the moisture still inside the bean, retaining the acidity. Light roasts also retain a bit more caffeine, believe it or not."

Playing with her hair.

"For French Roast, you let the beans roll right through the second crack, checking them with the d-dip every few seconds, looking for signs of moisture on the outside of the bean. Once you see enough moisture, which is really something you have to learn to recognize, then you d-drop them into the cooling tray. That can take another minute or two, at the most."

She glances over to the shop, waiting for the OPEN sign to flicker on, and it feels like she's looking right at me.

"Letting the second crack keep going is what gives d-darker coffee its earthiness. Some of the acids evaporate out producing that shiny look you watch for, and some of them form other more complex carbon chains within the bean. Along with this, some of the caffeine comes out, but not too much. So the longer you let the second crack go, the d-d-deeper the coffee's flavor gets. But if you wait too long the..." I have to clear my throat. "It'll burn, and you've wasted about three hundred bucks worth of coffee."

Jim whistles. "That much money for a bunch of beans?" Even behind his mop I can see his eyes light up.

"If you're lucky. Twelve bucks a pound is the low end, making a twenty-five pound batch worth about three hundred, yeah."

"So, the difference between light and dark roast is only, like, a minute?"

"More or less."

I hear a familiar muffled click followed by another, then another.

HOT JAVA
Roasted Fresh Every Morning!
Gallagher's
GOOD OLE CUP 'o' JOE
OPEN

Mona sits forward, finishing a paragraph then she slides out her bookmark, reading one last line, then slides it inside and closes her book.

"Well, we're up. Shelley should be here in a half hour. Why don't we head inside?"

"But didn't Lissa say we—"

"Yeah, well, I need some coffee."

Places everybody.

She crosses the street and is through the door and orders a Café Vienna and I haven't moved for nearly a minute. She's five and a half feet tall with long brown hair, hazel eyes and a smile that could melt me with one look but she's not looking my way, not yet, and I'm stuck in a weird sort of silence, like being on an airplane. It's not quiet but I can't hear anything.

"Hey, snap out of it, Roaster Boy. How the hell do I make a Café Vienna?"

"Sorry, right. M-m-m-make it like a latte, but p-put a spoonful of honey, real honey, and a bit of cinnamon before the espresso."

"Oh, okay." She dumps out the cup she was working on and starts over. In the same cup. I cringe.

"And real cinnamon, too, not that syrup flavoring shit."

"All. Right." She rolls her eyes.

Mona watches the exchange. Her expression drops, as if she's sorry she even came in.

"Then foam your milk and pull your shots. When the espresso is d- ah...when your shots are finished, stir them in so everything mixes, then pour in the milk and foam just like a latte."

Lissa glares at me. "Anything else, Roaster Boy?"

"Just, uh...sh-shake some cinnamon on top."

Dammit.

"Are you going to puh-puh-puh-pull through or what, Rainman?"

My face burns. "I'm fine. You get all that?"

"Sure, whatever. Do we even have real honey?"

"Just go study. Let me handle this."

I'm not about to let Mona's first drink here go horribly wrong. "Whatever."

She grabs her notebooks and heads to the back room. I grab a new mug and start over.

After an awkward pause, Mona speaks up. "I'm impressed. I

usually tell people all that, get a funny look and then settle for a vanilla latte."

Oh my God, her voice. It's better than I imagined. I know her face as well as I know my own, maybe better, but her voice is unbelievable.

"Coffee is what I d-do."

God. Fucking. Dammit.

She lowers her voice a little, saying, "How long have you been in the coffee business?"

"Couple years."

As I'm waiting for the espresso shot I watch as her hand moves toward mine, some suddenly foreign gesture. I stare at my own hand as if it weren't attached my body, like it's an alien object I couldn't possibly command.

"Mona."

Still, somehow, we shake hands, my fingers loose and rubbery. I let go and finish the drink, smiling, probably too much.

"Well, here you g-go. It's still p-pretty hot."

"Then it should keep me warm out there. Thank you."

She smiles and then she's gone, out the door and across the street and back to her spot. After hearing that lovely voice, the hours between right now and our next meeting suddenly become an eternity. Her voice echoes through my chest.

Mona. Mona. Mona.

* * *

Shelley comes through the door and the clock reads six-twenty-three. Seven minutes early, which is right on time for her but it means I must have been standing here for the better part of twenty minutes daydreaming. I try to act like I was busy with something as she hangs up her coat. Jim-Bo is over by the roaster sweeping to keep busy.

Shelley is a naturally happy, slightly introverted sort; pretty much the polar opposite of Lissa in every way imaginable, except looks. While she isn't Lissa's brand of plastic-pretty, Shelley has this subtle, librarian sort of sexy thing going on. You know what I mean; the type of girl who wears plain brown skirts with turtleneck sweaters, her hair always in a formless lump atop her head to keep it out of the way. Then one day, near closing time, you catch her taking off the plastic frame glasses, letting her hair down for a moment, rubbing the back of her neck. As her arms reach to put her hair back up her back arches, she goes into half a stretch, holds it; then you realize she's unbelievably attractive underneath it all and either confident enough not to flaunt it or completely unaware. Either way, it works. But don't go thinking I've got a thing for Shelley. I'm just reeling in the afterglow so compliments come easy at the moment.

"I'm gonna take off," Lissa squeaks as she darts over to the coat rack. "Huge test."

"Good luck." Shelley laughs.

"Laters."

"Wait, a test?"

"Summer school make-up test."

"On a Sunday? That's rough."

"More tips for us."

"You look happier than usual."

You have no idea.

"And nice pants. What's the occasion?"

"It's d-dif...ah, hard to explain."

10:

From across the park I spot the neon-clad pack forming in front of the main Asbury building right around eight o'clock. They're coming from every direction and by eight-fifteen the mob reaches critical mass and they're on the move. Every last one of them clutching a two-for-one coupon.

Shelley can't quite see all this from behind the counter so I get her attention and simply point. She leans forward, quizzically, then her eyes widen. I remind her what she said earlier, about more tips for us, but my stomach starts to twist a bit.

To Jim I say, "You'll be in charge of pastries." To Shelley, "You take the register and handle anything frozen since it's right there. I'll make the hot drinks. There shouldn't be too many cold drinks this early anyway."

They nod and I begin to shut down the roaster. As the mob moves through Elliot Park I look to Mona, her book already closed, standing and brushing any twigs and grass from her jeans, looking around for a quieter spot to read. In a moment she's gone.

The bell on the door jingles as Blue Glasses GEOFF waves people inside and instructs them to form a line that reaches outside, past the 'Maximum Capacity: 35 Persons' sign, all the way down the block and out of sight. GEOFF, he smiles huge and tells me they all need to get caffeinated before chapel.

"Wouldn't want to fall asleep, heh. But seriously, it's going to be great. It's a special service for new students and stuff." His blue-tinted eyes light up and he says, "You should try to get off work and come. It's gonna be great."

I take a look around at the line and then back to GEOFF.

"Shelley, you mind if I head over to chapel?"

"Well, I don't know, we might have to make some drinks for all these people."

GEOFF completely misses the sarcasm. He stands around making small talk as I make latte after vanilla latte. He introduces me to all the people he thinks I need to know. In the line up were Josh's number three, five, seven and eight, and some of his friends with other names. About half of Worship Live! comes through and their faces say, *No they do not remember me from yesterday.*

When the clock reads eight-forty-five and the line is still straggling outside GEOFF mentions that the chapel service starts at nine and we really need to pick up the pace a little. I'm speechless, but I think the look on Shelley's face drives the point home.

"Better get me a seat then, eh?"

He takes his sugar-free raspberry vanilla latte, with caramel on top, and makes a hasty exit. By nine-fifteen they're all gone. Some even left before getting through the line, the choice between caffeine and the Holy Ghost was too much. The shop once again falls into relative silence.

I fire up the roaster and as it roars back to life, the wall of sound restores my confidence that I'm awake. Mona was there, only a few feet away, and she spoke to me.

The rest of my shift blurs by until I find myself walking around the school. All I can remember is grabbing my backpack, headphones and an iced coffee, reading almost noon on the clock on my way out, but for some reason people are staring at me, so I slink away.

Another lap and I realize it takes less than ten minutes to walk around and through each of the three buildings that comprise Asbury University. My iced coffee is gone, my cell phone says one-thirty, so I must have walked through this place a dozen times, and with all this caffeine in me, probably at breakneck pace. I decide to wind down in the park for a while, but GEOFF, sans blue glasses, catches me off guard.

"Hey there, coffee guy. We're heading over to get refills. You game?"

"I'm trying to quit."

I make a break for home. This time last year I was invisible. I worked through the entire school year without ever knowing that there was a bubbly little Bible college only two blocks away. Not once had a single one of them walked up to me and told me about Jesus. I hadn't gotten any tracts on my door or windshield or anything. We'd peacefully co-existed. I roasted the coffee and made the drinks and put up with Eddie needing money every once in a while and I could handle all that.

These kids are everywhere and now I'm on their radar. I've put all this effort into blending in, it's hard not to feel suddenly exposed. Yet the biggest fear is that Mona, my apocalyptic muse, is one of them. For so long I've been hoping that she'll hold the answer, or at least some clue I can use, but maybe I've missed something all these years. Like trying to get the hidden message when you play old records backwards. Pink Floyd. The Beatles. Ozzy. Even if something is back-masked, even if there is a secret message, you have to be able to distinguish it from the rest of the meaningless noise.

These visions, some of them were hard to understand. Did I read into them too much? Did I miss the obvious looking only for what I wanted to see?

* * *

My stomach gets a knot and then my cell phone rings. This isn't intuition; it's just my luck.

Imagine all of Eddie's worldly possessions oozing out of the hatchback of my Honda, secured with a spiderweb of bungee cords and nylon rope.

"Hey man, this is Eddie. You around?"

"I answered, didn't I?"

"Well, uh...what's up?"

"What do you want?"

"Right, 'cause I called you. So... Look, I got this note on my door..." He pauses. "Dude...I didn't realize I was this far behind."

Picture my brother making breakfast tomorrow morning, in my kitchen, as a gesture of gratitude. This is what he calls Naked Eggs. Every time the grease pops, he...on second thought, don't picture that.

"You've got to be kidding. Exactly how far behind are you?"

"This note says six months."

"How long have you lived there?"

"Almost a year. Well..." I could hear him counting, "more like nine months. But this note says I have twenty-four hours to get my stuff out. Can they do that?"

"How should I know? Isn't this your line of work?"

"I repossess cars. This is different."

"My mistake."

I want to tell Eddie to call Dad, but Dad's got a countdown of his own going on: how many months left before his inheritance runs out and he has to find a job again. I think he's hoping to die first. Every time Eddie calls for money I can see Dad subtracting a week or two from his financial longevity.

I acquiesce.

"Give me a few minutes. I'll meet you where I dropped you off yesterday. Let's make this quick. I have somewhere to be around three."

"Wait, what?"

"You called because you need a place to stay."

"Oh, no, I thought you'd lend me some..."

"I'm working on a different strategy this time."

Keep your friends close and your idiots closer.

"Thanks, bro. Wow. Okay. Later."

And he's gone.

It's all becoming clear now. It's fate. I have an extra five-by-six foot room with a two-by-two foot closet and a tiny window that you'd never be able to crawl out of in the case of a fire (but that's why the rent is so cheap). My room has the only egress window in the entire lower level, but fire-code violations don't bother me. I knew when I signed the lease that I wasn't going to die in a fire. Trust me, I'd have seen that coming.

But somehow I also knew I'd need that second room. I could've taken the one-bedroom place across the street, same landlord, same distance to work. But I decided to pay an extra forty bucks a month for a second room, thinking maybe it'd be nice to have the extra space. Everything happens for a reason, I tell myself all the way to his place, everything happens for a reason.

Anything that doesn't fit in the hatchback we leave next to the dumpster, but that isn't much. Eddie didn't have a lot of stuff to begin with: a computer, a TV and a microwave, a couple beanbag chairs and some clothes stored in a pair of bluish Rubbermaid tubs. There's no furniture to pack. His computer sat on the box it came in. The TV was on the floor.

We bungee the hatchback down to the bumper and it won't close so we tie it off like a tourniquet. Eddie waves a solemn goodbye to his first apartment. His face says he's really going to miss the place. By the time we take off we'd run out of small talk, but the drive back had to be slow. I didn't want anything to fall out.

Except maybe Eddie.

* * *

Stomach knots. A momentary flash. The car swerves slightly and I make a decision. Detour.

"Hey, man, isn't your place that way?

"Trust me on this one."

I make a U-turn, careful not to lose any of that precious cargo, and head away from the nice part of town. I can't tell you where exactly, because I don't want to get tied up in the legal ramifications in case I happen to be still breathing when this finally gets out.

"This will be a valuable experience for you."

I tell him that when your betting record is as reputable as mine you get to meet a lot of people. Of course no one really knows who I am at the tracks, but Eddie doesn't have to know that. I simply say something is going down and I think it's worth checking out.

Turn by turn, it must look like I don't have a clue where I'm heading. Driving by feel is like that, but it saved Eddie's skin once so I'm not worried.

"I want you to know what you're getting mixed up in," I tell him as we pull off the main road onto little more than a pockmarked dirt path. We mosey past a handful of neglected warehouses and abandoned grain elevators until my rust bucket Honda reaches an old privacy fence topped with barbed wire. I put it in park and kill the engine.

Beyond the fence is a long dusty hill down to the Mississippi River. The sun's rays are hot and coming down hard, the river is low and brown, and there's nothing green in sight.

A large black Bronco pulls up followed by a maroon sedan, sending plumes of dust behind them that hang in the still air. Two men get out of each vehicle and walk about twenty yards toward the river. They form a sort of fraternal semicircle, each one lighting up a cigarette. Their faces are telling each other war stories, dirty jokes, complaining about women, drinking stories. I ask Eddie if any of those people look familiar. He keeps quiet but his face tells me I'm dead on.

After a few cigarettes their conversation ebbs. Finally, one guy pulls a key ring out of his pocket and aims it at the sedan. With a chirp the taillights blink and the trunk lid pops up and the four of them spread out. The one with the keys, he yells toward the car.

"You know the rules," he says a name I can't quite make out. Doesn't matter. By then, Eddie knows what's going to happen just as well as I do.

The four men stand fast, hands to their sides, waiting. From the trunk comes a muffled voice, shouting through a gag, hardly audible over the rush of the river. When his head appears, he shields his eyes from the sun with both hands because they're tied together. His face is a mess of black and blue and crusty dark brown.

The man with the keys shouts, "You got ten seconds once your feet hit the ground."

"Let's go."

I say nothing.

"I get the point, let's get out of here."

Another man speaks up. "I don't know, looks like he's chicken."

Then the man with the keys yells, "Don't think I'm going to put holes in Chester's upholstery because of you."

After a moment the man wiggles free of his gag enough to unleash a string of curse words as he tries to climb free of the trunk.

Eddie's eyes are fixed, fearful but unable to look away, and in that moment I realize how desensitized I've become. This guy is about to meet his maker and here I am hoping it doesn't take too long because I'm low on caffeine and I've got things to do.

The man falls back into the trunk.

"I've got places to be, kid." The ringleader scratches his head, indifferent, starts counting.

Ten, arms lead to shoulders as a beaten and bruised head emerges from the *Nine*, blackness of the trunk, like crawling out of the Devil's mouth. He flops *Eight*, onto the ground like a freshly caught fish, stunned, gasping for life. Spitting *Seven*, blood. With his tied hands, he pulls himself up on the bumper and steadies *Six*, his legs beneath him. He turns to face his four man firing squad, their *Five,* hands poised to pull out their guns, quick draw, like an old western shoot out. *Four,* the man limps left, right, looking for an escape route. His head turns right *Three,* toward the river, like maybe he could swim for it. He looks to his hands, tied. Not a *Two,* chance. He bolts away from the four men and toward the front of the car, but then *One and a half,* a man who even Eddie and I hadn't seen pops up from in front of the car *One,* and smiles with one eye open, the way you have to smile when you're aiming a hand gun *Zero,* right at someone's chest, arm fully extended *Bang.*

The hostage stumbles back and the fifth man, I'm assuming it's Chester, motions with his head for the men to move toward the river. They close in and begin taking silenced shots at his knees, each followed by a reddish puff. The man falls.

On his back now, they shoot one arm, the other, then Chester holds his hand up while the bound man is still moving. He kneels down, putting his face next to the man's ear like he's telling him a secret, then pats him on the chest. At that, the four men stow their weapons and pick the dying man up by his hands and feet and heave him back and forth as he yells a very labored, *Wait.* They swing him back and forth and he screams, *I'm not dead yet!* A split second before he hits the water the man gets out a final, *Nooo—*

The men stand around to watch. All except Chester. He's wiping his hands on a white handkerchief, already getting back in the car. The muddy Mississippi rages on as a man I've never met spends his last few seconds of life struggling to keep his bludgeoned head above water.

Eddie is more than a little dazed, but he doesn't say a word. He doesn't need to. His face says he knew those people, especially the drowning man.

11:

Getting Eddie and his junk back to my place quickly turns into part two of this morning's nightmare. Yesterday students were moving in all throughout the day so traffic was heavy but manageable. Today it seems everyone had the same idea – go to church in the morning, then race over at the last possible minute.

So Eddie and I pull up about two blocks away from campus to find ourselves in the thick of it, blending right in with the seemingly endless line of cars packed to the hilt with clothes and beanbag chairs and computers.

But the kicker is this: as we're about to make the second to last turn, not even a hundred yards from my place at that T-inter-section right in front of Gallagher's, someone coming from the other direction takes a hasty left and misjudges the space their twenty-foot trailer would require to make the corner. Honestly, I have no idea who would need that much stuff for their dorm, but they catch the bumper of a parked car and drag it about six feet before losing momentum. They're locked up.

I punch my horn in disgust, but that's a bad idea. Imagine a chorus of at least two dozen different horns sounding out two or three notes, all within a quarter step of each other but not quite right, blaring, sustaining, out of tune.

The driver and a couple teenage girls climb out to survey the damage. Three or four other people are out of their cars on cell phones, gesturing as they talk as if that might make it more clear to the people on the other end. In the distance you can hear the wave of horns move through the gridlock, along with the occasional shriek of tires followed by a crunch.

The police show up, then a tow truck, each making their way to the scene by driving through Elliot Park. As the tow-truck driver and the cops are deciding the best way to resolve the traffic jam, my lack of AC becomes problematic. I kill the engine, get out and we take a seat on the hood. Eddie follows suit.

The chorus of horns, still reaching a crescendo in the distance, is underscored by the clunk of engines shutting off and the sound of dozens of car doors opening and shutting as the traffic jammed students all begin getting out of their cars. When you watch the nature channel, how a school of fish moves instantaneously, changing directions in unison; this is the closest human equivalent I've ever seen.

A couple guys in a pickup take the next step, pulling out lawn chairs to kick back on the sidewalk. Others begin to crank up their stereos, and a few start up a game of Frisbee in the park.

Like an angel, Shelley comes out of Gallagher's with a couple iced coffees.

"Thought that was you. Looks like you'll be here a while."

"It's almost three. Aren't you supposed to be off by now?"

"That new girl, Laura, just remembered she has to move back to school today."

"Genius. Wow."

"Yeah. U of M's classes start tomorrow, too. But don't worry. Lissa's going to close for her tonight. You know, since she stiffed us this morning."

"How'd you manage that?"

"I have my ways," she smiles, a tiny sparkle behind those boring glasses.

"So is it busy, or did the mob use all their coupons this morning?"

"We've had more than our average three customers an hour this afternoon, but it's nothing I can't handle."

I nod to the accident. "Truck clipped a parked car, now they're stuck."

"Sunday drivers."

"Oh, wow." I roll my eyes.

"Wow what?"

"Only the worst pun of the year, that's all."

"I don't hear you cracking anyone up."

"I get paid to make coffee."

"Maybe I'm branching out, trying to bring people some joy."

"What brings more joy than coffee?" I wiggle the cup.

She brushes away a lock of windblown hair, tucks it behind her ear.

"Honestly, though. Thanks for the drinks. Really."

"And the laugh." Eddie chimes in, far too glib, obviously trying to flirt. I try to elbow him into shutting his mouth, but he makes it obvious, says, "Ouch," elbows me back. Shelley's blushing and looking for an exit. I try to help her save face, change the subject.

"You know, I bet some of these people could use a drink."

"And I could certainly use the tips."

"If any of them actually leave one, that is. I'm sure Allison bitched about how little we made last night."

"Must've been rough."

"Well it can't hurt to try."

I stand up on the hood and address the masses, hands to my mouth like a megaphone.

"Hot as Hell out here, isn't it?"

People look up, some nod, but most don't notice, so I try again.

"I said, it's hot as Hell out here, isn't it?"

People start to look. I hear one parent say something about watching my language and I chuckle to myself. One of the cops instinctively puts his hand to his waist and locks eyes with me.

"Well, for the next half hour, all cold drinks at Gallagher's are twenty-five percent off."

I gesture dramatically towards the shop. People's heads turn. At first the group is hesitant, but a low murmur begins sweeping through the crowd until one guy jumps up from his lawn chair.

"Well alright, brother."

Masses of people begin moving toward the door. I sit back

down next to Eddie the moment he spews his first sip all over the windshield. He looks at me, his voice a strained whisper.

"This is the worst iced latte I've ever had."

"That's because it's not an iced latte. It's iced coffee. Big difference."

"Well, whatever you want to call it, it tastes like it came out of a dead dog's ass."

"Iced *lattes* are for girls. This is a man's drink. This..." I hold up the cup so the beads of sweat sparkle in the sun, "...this beverage is brewed for twenty-four hours, and it's brewed cold. It has a lot more caffeine and a much stronger flavor than pretty much anything else out there."

"More caffeine, eh?"

"Much more. So if you don't like it, add some sugar or something."

He takes a long sip followed by a scowl that would make you think it was low-grade moonshine.

"I think I'm gonna have to. Sugar, I mean."

It takes the tow-truck operator and two policemen about a half hour to separate the vehicles without causing too much more damage. The owner of the car still hasn't shown up, so now they're working on paperwork because the front tire is flat and looks like the axel may have broken as well.

The hood flexes beneath Eddie and me as we occasionally shift around, getting as comfortable as possible.

"So, she's nice." Eddie has that hint of wasted optimism in his voice again.

"Shelley? Yeah. She's great." My voice is flat.

"She available?"

"Aren't you practically engaged?"

"Not anymore." Suddenly I wish I hadn't asked, but he goes on. "She took off with some guy from the U of M. Found out a couple days ago."

And I'm supposed to say, "What's he got that you don't?"

"A car, I guess."

And probably a place to live, a real job, a high-school diploma, a bank account that's not in the negative half the time. A right hand. I have to bite my tongue.

"Well, you really ought to take a break from girls for a while. You're on the rebound."

"Yeah." He sighs.

We overhear the cops saying how cars are backed up for at least a mile in both directions with four or five fender benders blocking the two intersections they'd have used to bleed the gridlock to the east. One highway exit is backed up all the way to the previous exit.

Eddie and I watch the tow truck pull the mangled car away through the park and then the police are asking people to get back in their cars so a traffic cop can blow her whistle at us to go ahead and make the turn. It's only now I realize my radio's been on for over an hour now so I sweat a bit when the engine hesitates. It starts. A few minutes later we're back at my place, the chorus of horns picking up again as the cars that were rerouted start coming face to face with the newly freed flow of traffic from our side. I'm just relieved to be out of the fray as even my street turns into a parking lot.

I clear a path through the apartment while Eddie unloads all his junk and brings it down. As small as that second room is, everything of his pretty much fits inside.

The apartment looks like a larger, messier version of the room we used to share, but in my defense, it smells a little better. To get to my apartment you walk through the building's laundry room and the lady on the first floor uses more than enough fabric softener and drier sheets to keep my place smelling alpine fresh. We order pizza that night and each of us kills a six-pack of Coors Light.

"I still can't believe you like this stuff. It's like beer-flav—"

"I know, I know, beer-flavored water. Do we have to go over

this every single time?"

He giggles a wet-sounding burp out of the way and says, "Yes, as a matter of fact, we do."

"He says as he finishes one off and reaches for another."

He looks contemplative for a moment, then nods. "Too-Chi."

"Don't you mean touché?"

"Grassy ass."

"What?"

"That means, Yes."

"Gracias means, Thank you."

"No, man. Thank *you*."

"Keep on drinking, buddy. I need all the advantage I can get."

We spend hours slaughtering scads of awful creatures in this amusingly graphic first-person shooter video game, something about zombies. Games where you use a gun instead of a normal controller are the only kind he can play these days, so he's damn good.

Sometime later, between umpteenth blood-spewing rounds, Eddie leans over to say, "It could be worse. [Hic] Least Dad doesn't need a place to stay."

"Wow. You can say that again."

"Hey, you know what?" he slurs. "Do you have any eggs?"

"Sure, I guess."

"I'll make you breakfast tomorrow. I have this thing—"

"No, wait, shit. Come to think of it, I'm out of eggs."

"Oh, okay. Then I'll make you a bowl of cereal. The best fucking bowl of cereal you ever tried."

Later, as Eddie teeters on the edge of drunken slumber, I throw out the half dozen eggs I had left in the fridge. Just in case.

* * *

Monday morning comes fast and hard and my dream is mostly back to normal. Mona and I are sharing a cup of coffee, I'm no longer confessing to murder, and then fade to white and then nothing.

The difference is that this time the pulsing of the alarm clock is more like the beeping of a cement truck backing over my head. The echo remains long after I've beaten the plastic clock into submission.

I'm seriously hung-over, so I count the cans. Two, four, six, eight, nine...ten...twelve... I eventually hit eighteen. Shit. I stumble around, making coffee and getting dressed, and then I step on Eddie.

Eddie?

The previous day's events flood back into my still awakening, slightly confused mind and I realize that, no, this is not a dream. I can hear him snoring, and sound means reality. He rolls over onto the open pizza box but doesn't wake up.

I'm out the door before I have a second chance to wake him up. The crisp morning air tries to rattle me out of my stupor, but my brain is pulsating like a strobe light.

When I get to work the thought of roasting coffee with all the noise and heat sounds about as fun as taking a rusty dentist drill to an open wound in a bathtub full of lemon juice. I click on as few lights as possible, remove the access plate, but the noise of the shop-vac is too much and I hurl into a fake plant.

"Well, that's fine," David's voice crackles out of my cell phone. "Come to think of it...have you ever called in before?"

"No, I guess not."

"Yeah, what's it been, a year and a half? Almost two. Okay, well stick around until Elise gets there."

"You mean Lissa."

"Right. Whatever the flavor of the month is now. I guess her keys were stolen yesterday."

"Really?"

"Yeah. At church, of all places."

I try not to laugh at the thought of Barbie Manson sitting

through a church service.

"Anyway," David goes on, "I'll have a new key made today or tomorrow."

"Sounds good."

"So, how'd you do the other day, at Canterbury?"

"Not too bad. You win some, you lose some."

"That so? From what I hear you do pretty well."

"Really?" My insides begin to turn.

"Yeah. Word is there's this punk-rocker kid, wears these big headphones, does pretty well for himself."

"Well, I can't complain." My stomach began to eat itself from the inside.

"Well, feel better, Zeek." He knows a lot more than he's letting on, I can tell.

"Thanks."

click

The door rattles. Lissa is knocking. The clock says she's only a few minutes late, which is pretty good. The moment she's inside I tell her I'm sick and squeeze past. She tries to launch into a bitch fit but the door jingles shut. I wave and stumble away.

Not having to deal with her helps my overall mood until I remember the new roommate situation. Suddenly home doesn't seem like such a refuge. Coffee isn't taking the edge off the hangover, either.

I cross the street and my peripheral catches a glimpse of someone familiar. She's walking across the park, book in hand, looks as if she's heading directly for me. She's not. She finds a spot next to her tree and settles in to read.

Such a shame, when the OPEN sign flickers on she'll be at Allison's mercy. As much as I hate the idea of Mona having to deal with that this early in the morning, it's the slightly better of two evils for me. With my head splitting, what I must smell like after last night's binge, it's definitely not the right time to make a second impression.

Back at the apartment Eddie's still sleeping and I have no idea if or when he needs to get to work. Screw him. I need to shower off last night's residue and get some rest. Eddie can fend for himself.

The shower is hot and the room fogs up thick and heavy, my motions feel slow and labored, the pounding of the water is on the verge of making me nauseous, and all the steam makes it hard to breathe; altogether not unlike the first time I heard Mona's voice, except that was a good type of overwhelming, this is quite the opposite.

When I finally towel off, my head's spinning so bad I can't even come up with a decent metaphor. I grab for my journal and see three of them, toss them every which way toward the many area rugs that are cropping up below me, aim for the most convincing idea of where my bed should be and crash. I close my eyes and dream of Hell.

* * *

The highway might be scenic if it weren't so cold. Still, this is new. Naked trees stand gaunt and black against a muted sky. Everything else is grey and formless, a landscape worn smooth, made destitute by the bitter cold and a dry, breath-sucking wind. By the time I make the trip, Hell will be all but frozen over.

I'm driving, checking the map, eating leftover fries, wearing gloves with the fingers cut out. My breath clouds the glass as I breathe into my hands one at a time.

Now I'm sure you're wondering, so I'll get this out of the way now. There are two basic versions of how Hell got its name.

The first holds that a pair of German travelers stepped out of a stagecoach one sunny afternoon in the 1830s, and one said to the other, "So schön und hell!" – roughly translated as, "So beautiful and bright!" Some locals overheard the comment and the name stuck.

The second, more interesting story holds that after Michigan gained statehood in 1841, George Reeves, the town's founder, was asked what he thought the town should be called.

The town was small then and it's small now, a little under three hundred people. The only thing it seemed to have going in its favor back then was a mill, also founded by George Reeves. At some point it became tradition to have the first bushel of wheat threshed each year taken to George's distillery to be made into whiskey.

Then George opened a tavern. Soon, the story goes, horses would come home without riders, wagons without drivers. If someone asked a woman where her missing husband was, she'd throw her arms up in the air and say, "Oh, he's gone to Hell!"

When asked what he thought the town should be called, George Reeves replied, "You can call it Hell for all I care. Everyone else does."

One way or another the name became official on October 13, 1841. Of course I wasn't dreaming all these trivial details, only of the drive, stopping for directions, et cetera.

In addition to the original general store, which the Internet says is still there to this day, Hell has a motorcycle dealership and an ice-cream shop. In my dream I ask someone at the ice-cream shop for directions and they oblige. I've never dreamed of Hell before, which is unsettling. If this town is a part of my future, why hasn't it ever been a part of my past?

My subconscious's newfound interest in Hell becomes clear as I see myself standing at the front door of an old house, and as the front door opens Mona stands before me, a bright silhouette in a beam of wavering light as if from a fireplace. She leans against the doorway, and in typical dreamtime it takes forever to approach. She touches my hand, fingers poking out of cut off gloves, but the gloves go up my arms like gauze, her perfect cheek is bruised, my movements are slower than normal, labored, and my stomach sinks because none of this is right. Still, she appears to be nothing but happy to see me, and then the stench of burning meat tears me away from Hell before we reach our final act; coffee, books, fade to white.

* * *

From the smell of things Eddie is busy charring the last of my breakfast links. I only hope he's not as naked as he sounds. The louder the grease pops, the louder he yelps. I peek out my door and he's in a pair of boxers, so at least God doesn't totally hate me.

"Hey man, I thought you went to work," he mumbles through a mouthful of I don't know what.

"I did, then I came back. Shouldn't you be at work?"

"I called in, told them my uncle died. Only I left out that it happened like, eight years ago. Got three days off for it, man."

"Very grown up."

"P.S. You're out of cereal."

"Noted. Thanks for not being naked, by the way."

"Oh, man, I don't do that anymore. I figure it's not worth the risk." He looks down and jiggles around under his boxers, like maybe I don't get the joke. Then he goes for the clencher. "So, you want some sausage?"

"Ugh."

I slam the door and throw on some clothes, saying, "I can't stay for breakfast. I need to get over to the school."

"Classes already?"

"No, I'm meeting someone."

Grease pops and he shouts, "What?"

"Meeting someone!"

"You should get some eggs, man! I learned how to make these amazing omelets; it's my new specialty. You know, since I gave up on Naked Eggs. Oh, and tell your girlfriend 'hi' for me."

"Sure thing."

"So she is your girlfriend."

"Shut up."

"I'm just saying—Ow!"

"I've only known her for a day or so."

"Wait, what?"

"What?"

"Who are you talking about?"

"Who the Hell are you talking about?"

"Shelley."

"Dude, you're on the rebound, remember? Give it a rest."

"Wait, then who *are* you talking about?"

"No one."

"Aw, Zeek's got a crush."

"Bye."

I grab my backpack and headphones and take off. And though Eddie has done nothing particularly annoying this morning—he did attempt to make me a not-so-naked breakfast—still, he's somehow grating on me. I need to relax.

I'm searching my iPod for something to fit the bill—Depeche Mode, maybe some downtempo Nine Inch Nails—but I stop dead in my tracks in front of a jet black '68 Mustang. Tinted windows, lake pipes, matte-black wheels, dice in the mirror.

And you've got to be fucking kidding me. Michigan plates. My face reflects in the near liquid finish, a jet-black mirror, with the brightness of mid-day over my shoulder and in the distance, heavy clouds approaching, come to black out the sun.

12:

I'm not sure where I'm going. I can't find the Hawaiian-themed tour map and I wasn't really listening when JOSHUA showed me around. I head for the main building and try not to appear lost.

The place is buzzing with new kids looking for their next opportunity to be the center of attention and older students observing the process from the safety of their little cliques. The pecking order is being sorted out in real time.

I'm looking for the deli, and not only because I'm starving. That's where I'll see Mona next. Then I think, the halls are buzzing, the whole place is alive, people literally everywhere. That means I'm late. I'm a day late. This was supposed to happen yesterday, Sunday, before the rush to campus. The halls are supposed to be mostly empty.

Fuck.

I make my way to the deli and my mind jolts into full alert the way I always do when I expect something to finally happen. It's not a sense worth fighting. As I walk past the entrance some guy was supposed to ask me to watch the counter while he got change from downstairs and then she was going to pass by on her way to the Financial Aid office. And I have to tell myself that's the past now. I'm late.

I look around and probably make it a little too obvious that I'm not sure where the line starts. From across the room Joshua (sans nametag) hails me like a cab.

"Zeek! Hey! Buddy!" He's behind the cereal bar, but most people are amassed around the sandwich counter. I nod imperceptibly and consider making a dash for the skyway. It's too late, eye contact has been established, I'm stuck.

"Zeek, buddy. You pay for laundry, right?"

"What?"

I cross the crowded room quick as I can to keep him from

shouting and drawing any more attention, though it's probably too late for that.

"You live in an apartment." He nods like he's telling me something I don't know.

"Yeah."

"So I assume you pay for laundry." His voice keeps trailing up at the end like it's some sort of remedial question.

"Well, yeah."

"In quarters."

"Yes. In quarters." Get to the point, for Christ's sake.

"So my question to you is, do you have any quarters? We're totally out."

"No. Fresh out."

"That's cool. Can you watch the counter for a sec? I gotta go grab some change from downstairs." He's already heading down the hall. "Oh, and we're on tonight at Gallagher's. I signed us up."

"Great." I yell after him as sarcastic as possible. This doesn't make any sense. "By the way, d- ah... You know where the Financial Aid office is?"

"I thought you were paying for school yourself." He disappears down the hall.

It was worth a shot.

Given the mass of people in the room, it's obvious Joshua's been hard pressed to find someone to watch the counter for him, and now the pecking order has shifted and I can feel the flock associating me, that new kid with the headphones, the one that stutters, with Joshua. Guilt by association. In nothing flat I've once again gone from unknown to outcast.

And now Mona makes her appearance and I want to die. She probably heard the entire thing, sitting in the far corner of the room, leaned back into one of those hotel-furniture-style chairs in the study area. She picks up a red travel mug and walks toward me. It all feels wrong but there's no way to get out of it. I rest my bag on the counter and try to look cool, to lean like I know what I'm doing. I try not to meet her eyes to soon.

"So, Mr. Café Vienna." I try to smile without overdoing it, and she says, "Remember me?"

I snap my fingers in that remembering-someone's-name sort of way and she smiles.

"Mona, right?"

"That's me." She smiles.

I start to sweat. What is it? Is there something on my shirt? In my teeth? What's she waiting for?

"This is the part where you tell me your name."

"Right. Yeah. E-z-z-z-e-z-z uhm...E-z-ZEEK-iel." God. Dammit. "People call me Zeek," comes out rapid fire, like I've got tourettes or something.

"Ezekiel. Okay. Don't feel bad."

"What?"

"I noticed that guy kind of blindsided you there. He did the same to me yesterday. I guess the deli runs out of change a lot."

"Oh. Okay."

"Well, I was looking for Financial Aid, too. Mr. Number One was more than happy to show me around yesterday, so maybe when he gets back I can show you where it is."

I have to look away, afraid my eyes will give away the mix of anxiety and excitment, but it turns. Despite the warm invitation, I'm reeling with anger. I'm actively working on my poker face because in my head I see my hands clamping down around Joshua's beating heart. How the Hell did I miss this? I was supposed to meet her here. I was supposed to walk around with her, get to know her, in a nice quiet deli, down a nice quiet hallway. That was mine. My future and my eventual memory.

As quickly as it rose this fury turns from Joshua to Eddie. Maybe I'd have been here yesterday if I'd just told Eddie to fend for himself and find his own place. I'm not my half-brother's keeper. So what if he got evicted? He's got as many ways of finding money as he does of losing it.

But how is any of this possible?

Ever since I made my third-grade teacher walk into the path of a stray bullet I decided not to mess with the future, to just let things happen. What if even that was wrong? Or worse, what if my dreams have been warnings all along? Not signs that I'm heading in the right direction, but apocalyptic visions of what will happen if I go the wrong way?

With my stomach gnawing itself again, the floodgates of doubt open within my mind. The very foundation of my most basic assumption is crumbling under the pressure of the unknown.

I could cry.

"You still with me?"

Clearing my throat, "Oh, mmm hmm. Yeah. Sorry."

She pauses, a skeptical glance, then goes on. "Anyway, Joshua gave me a tour of the campus, but I wasn't really paying attention. He sort of bugs me."

She smiles and her eyes blaze like an ocean sunrise, deep blue and on fire and just like that I'm back in the moment. She keeps talking but all I can hear is the tide of doubt moving down, rushing away, subsiding. When Joshua gets back, patting me on the back like we're old friends, Mona loops her arm through the bend of my elbow and says, "Shall we?"

The way she tilts her head, it falls into a column of light from the window.

"You know, you're lucky in a way. Paying as you go."

"Oh, you heard?"

"I think everyone heard."

"Things really get around this place, I guess."

"Yes they do. Anyway, my mom, she set up this college savings account for me, but only if I went to school here," she rolls her eyes, "you know, like she did about a hundred years ago, and wh— Sorry. You don't need to hear my life's story."

Her arm is tight against the inside of my elbow.

"Oh no, it's fine. So...you're not into this whole—"

"Bible-college thing. No, it's not that."

She gets lost in a thought.

"Where d-did you want to go to school?" Damn stutter.

"I don't know, a normal university, a state college, whatever. I've hardly thought about it because this has always been the plan. At least this place is accredited now, so classes will transfer elsewhere. I figure I'll do a couple years of general credits here, then transfer to the U of M or something and just suck it up."

"What are you going t-t-to major in?" Dammit. What the fucking fuck?

She stops walking. Shit. Was that out loud? I'm staring at the ground like the first time my step-mom heard me cuss, but she doesn't say anything and I have to break the crushing silence.

"What is it?"

"Pardon me for being...forward, but you shouldn't worry about it. About...you know."

"Worry about what?" I'm sweating blood at this point, but I finally manage to bring my eyes up to hers.

"When you..." she tips her head down, an apology. "When you miss a syllable, or whatever, you can see it all over your face."

My face is hot. A stone slides down my throat. Not this conversation. Not now. Not so soon. I've been through it a million times but I thought I had a few days.

"Hey, all I'm saying is, no one would notice if you didn't make it obvious."

She pulls on my arm. It's too much, how familiar she seems to treat me, the smalltown manners, but with a straightforward honesty that should be disarming. I'm caught completely off guard, which is something I'm not used to and don't much like.

"I'm sorry, Ezekiel. I said too much. I'm always doing that." Her arm loosens slightly. "Look, the office is—"

"No."

I close my elbow so she can't pull her arm out of mine, which comes as a surprise to us both. We lock eyes for a long moment and she studies my face. I rethink my move and loosen my elbow again. She stays.

A moment.

Then I say, "Shall we?"

She nods. We walk on.

"Who knows? Maybe psychology."

"What?"

"You asked about my major. Maybe psychology. Right now I work in the children's ward at United Mercy. I love working with children, so maybe child psychology. Or Sign Language. I know a little, and there are some really great opportunities working with deaf children.

"Besides, it'll be a while before I have to decide for good, and you're supposed to change it once or twice anyway. Figure I'll major in Greek for at least a semester, just to throw people off.

"Funny thing is," she continues after a thoughtful pause, "half these girls here, they'll never pick a major at all. They're here for their M-R-S degree."

"Is that a Bible thing?"

She laughs. "They want to be pastor's wives. M-R-S They're here to scope out the prospects. Most aren't planning to graduate with anything more than an associate's degree in the Bible, a ring on their finger and a kid on the way. 'Ring by spring or your money back.' That's the motto."

"I had no idea."

"Last night my floor had a sort of meet-and-greet time. I was one of the few who actually watched the movie and tried to ignore the giggling over all the cute pastoral majors. Even Number One back there has a couple fans."

"Okay, n-now I know you're joking."

"Nope. His dad is the senior pastor at some mega-church

down in Houston, something like four- or five-thousand people. He knows once he graduates, he'll pretty much write his own ticket wherever he goes.

"Well, here we are." But her arm stays intertwined with mine. "And...they're closed."

There's a note on the door saying that someone should be back in thirty minutes, but it doesn't say when that thirty minutes started.

"Well, at least now I know where it is. Thanks for the walk."

"Yeah, any time. Speaking of time..." She pulls out a pink cell phone. "Yep. I've got a plane to catch, so I need to go pack."

"D-didn't you just get here?" Dammit.

"I'm visiting my grandmother in Arizona for a few days. Ever been to Phoenix?"

"Nope."

"Well it's basically hot all the time. All in all, as unfortunate as it may seem, I might have to miss the first day of class."

"Well that sounds awful." I smile, more and more relieved that things haven't been totally thrown off track.

"I'm sure I'll make due. See you around, Ezekiel."

As her arm moves free of mine, she drags her fingers along the inside of my elbow and it's a good thing I'm only inches from the wall. I coolly lean back to steady myself, cover by saying, "Guess I'll wait here, then."

Mona pauses, puffs her long bangs away from her mouth, thinks to say something, thinks better of it, then turns away.

I find myself sitting on a bench in the park, collecting my thoughts. I hate to see her leave, it feels like a heart attack, but in all honesty I could use a little time to make sense of things. Did I know she was leaving?

My cell phone buzzes. I take one look at the caller ID and hit the reject button. It's that weirdo from the other day and I don't need any more complications.

I imagine dingy lipstick residue caked onto the mouthpiece of an old-fashioned rotary phone, wondering why poor Mr. Ezekiel doesn't answer.

Phone buzzes again. Same number. I hit reject and turn the thing off. He'll get the picture sooner or later.

When I remember Eddie is at my place I decide to take the long way home. Which is to say, I walk aimlessly for about an hour, only changing directions when the batteries in my MP3 player die. As I near my block, the '68 Mustang I'd admired earlier has roared to life. It flies past and a distinctly feminine hand waves, AC/DC blaring from the open windows. She rounds the corner and screams toward the highway. And I feel like I should have known all along, which is unsettling when knowing all along is what you're used to.

13:

Home again. Eddie's gone, which is good. But he's managed to break my coffee pot, which is a fucking Greek tragedy. I'm not desperate enough to head back to work for coffee, so since Mona is out of town for a few days I sleep the afternoon away.

Maybe I'll have a new dream. One where Mona and I don't meet in a book-filled room and then fade to white and then nothing. Or at least a dream that gives me a clue about when she gets back from Arizona, or if anything else has changed. But the time passes in dark silence until I jolt out of bed to a crashing sound somewhere outside.

I race up the stairs and out the door only to come within inches of breaking my neck as I barrel into Eddie sitting like a lump on the porch. I sprawl headlong on the grass, slide a few feet, then double over to catch my breath.

"You're not having a seizure, are you, dude? 'Cause I ain't cleaning you up at this point."

I can't draw enough breath to say what comes to mind so I flip him the bird.

It's quiet for a moment while my lungs find their shape again. The sky is nearly dark now and the wind is noticeably cooler than the last few days. I roll onto my back. Night is falling, so I did sleep. No dreams. Weird.

"What are you doing out here, man?"

Something crunches under the back of my heels. I sit up. Broken glass has piled up along the end of the driveway and the recycle bin is almost empty.

"I don't know. I got bored. I was gonna have a smoke, but I can't find my lighter." He throws another bottle.

"That'll be great next time I have to mow the lawn. Since when do you smoke, anyway?"

"Since Jennifer left me."

"All of two days now. I bet you've got cancer already. Congratulations."

"Nearly three days. Anyway, it's wicked cold out here." He tosses a final bottle that misses the pavement and bounces across the grass into the fence.

The door shuts and his footfalls fade into the basement. There must be clouds on the horizon. Long shafts of light shoot out above the roofline. There's a spectacular sunset happening somewhere but I can't seem to pull myself up off the lawn.

* * *

I wrote a lot that night but eventually fell asleep. The next couple days blurred by. Tuesday, Eddie moped around the apartment, stuffing his face, drinking and shooting zombies, taking regular trips outside to nurse his new habit, all the while I was preoccupied with thoughts of Mona. It's surprisingly difficult getting to know someone you've known for nine and a half years. I wrote all day, trying not to lose any of the things I hadn't expected. The new stuff. I searched online about Hell, Michigan, and tried to find the deeper connection, if any existed. Google. Wikipedia. Yahoo! Answers. Anything. As if the collected knowledge on the Internet would somehow hold a clue that I'd overlooked. Sometimes I found myself sitting for hours, replaying the memory of her voice saying my name, hoping I wasn't changing it over time the way old mixtapes eventually wear thin and distort.

In the shower Wednesday morning I noticed that all the weeds outside the tiny bathroom window had frosted to the glass. I pulled out my winter coat and went to work where I cranked up some grimier Tom Waits tunes loud enough to discourage conversation with any Asbury students that might venture inside. When that didn't work I reverted to my typical anti-social music, Nine Inch Nails, though this was a risk should David stop by. He didn't. I spent the afternoon shopping for a new coffee-maker and trying to stay warm. My landlord's policy was that the heat wouldn't be turned on until the weather hit a certain temperature for a certain number of days in a row. No one knew what that magic number was, but he swore it was legal. On the brink of huddling together for warmth, Eddie got the idea to go out and buy a space heater.

Thursday morning I woke up knowing that I was supposed to go to classes that day and Mona wouldn't be around, which felt like being thrown to the wolves. I pictured it like an intervention, only instead of drugs or alcohol they'd be asking me to stop my swearing, toss out my unholy concert shirts and for the love of God, burn all those evil rock-and-roll records. They did this with new members of the youth group all the time growing up, which is why I rarely went.

With coffee brewing and Eddie back at work I had the place to myself. I tried to picture Mona sitting poolside in a retirement community in Arizona, sipping iced tea as her grandmother sits reading or knitting or whatever old women in Phoenix do. I imagined Mona smiling, talking about this strange boy she met who wears headphones and stutters.

There was no reason to think she'd be thinking of me at all, but it kept me distracted from my clouded breath and the growing splinters of ice reaching across all the garden-level windows.

* * *

I wake up Friday knowing that I have to work in the morning then go to a couple classes in the afternoon where I'll at least be in the same room as Mona, then I have to head out to Canterbury and make my picks; all in time to take Mona on a sunset walk along the river, and all the while trying to avoid Eddie. My gut says to keep my distance from him today, but he corners me while I'm still at work.

"Zeek, dude, you gotta come and check this out. You ever see a car get repossessed?"

"I'd love to, but I have to get to class."

"No way, man, you gotta see this. It's one of those brand new Cadillacs. It's right in front of the shop, just down eleventh a bit."

"Wait, what? B-back up a little."

"Okay, so I'm heading to work and I notice this silver Cadillac XLR. You know the convertible hard top one? Only this one is super rare. It's a V-series, man. They go for a hundred G's on the fucking nose. Most dealers only get one of them so most people had to special order one."

Oh shit.

"Anyway, one of the cars I've been trying to repo just happens to be a V-series XLR. There hasn't been a single payment made on it, you know. Just the initial money down and the dealer warranty. So I see this car, the VIN number matches, and the guy's even got personalized plates that say ZOOM. This fucking guy has been my Achilles' tendon for nearly three months."

"Heel, Eddie. It's Achi—"

"Fuck it, man. Heel. Speak. I'll roll over if you want me to. I'm so fucking excited."

Eddie drags me along but I already know where this is heading.

"They're gonna send the flatbed over and load up the car up and wait for him to show. Gary's drafting a bunch of paperwork that will basically work like a warrant, ordering him to give up his other cars—that's right, C-A-R-S, plural—or to get them all paid up immediately. You have to come and watch, man. It's gonna be sick."

I grab his shoulder, "Man...that's my boss's car."

"What?"

"You're looking for a guy who has a bunch of coupes, right? An RX-8, a Honda 2000, a brand-new Vette, an M3, that new

Cadillac..." I trail off in disbelief. Eddie's eyes widen.

"Yeah, dude. That's your boss? David Gallagher is your boss? I mean, I'm not really supposed to even say his name. I could get in trouble for telling you, but shit man. David Fucking Gallagher. That's your boss?"

I breathe into my hands. "If he's that far behind on his cars, I'm wondering about Gallagher's?"

"Huh?"

"Do me a favor. Can you find out if there's anything out against the coffee shop? I don't really know what it would be called." Suddenly I'm worried about my job when I should be worried about whether I'll be around to see it collapse. First-world problems.

"Oh...oh, right. That would be in a different area, but I know a couple people in private banking. If anything's going down, that's probably where it would be."

That explains all the promotions, I guess.

"Let me make a couple calls for you, I'll see what I can find out. But from the looks of the accounts I do have access to, I'd say it's not a bad idea to start looking for a new job."

"Fuck, Eddie. Just...fuck."

"Don't shoot the messenger. I'm just saying, almost every account he has ends up overdrawn every month. I mean four figures overdrawn. When the first of the month comes up, he'll be positive for a week. Ten days tops."

Eddie reaches out and pats my shoulder, and for a moment I forget everything I hate about him and really appreciate the gesture.

The cold wind finds its way through my winter coat, up the sleeves, under the waist, and it tightens around my ribs like a fist. I skip class and head straight to Canterbury. If things are that bad with the shop I need to make sure I have money to live on.

It's not so much the idea of losing a source of income as the fact that I really like the job. It's been my first niche in life where

I stood on my own two feet. I belonged. I had a handful of people who came from across town to buy a pound of coffee I roasted, even if they didn't really know who I was beyond my job title. It felt good.

In my reverie, I make it to the tracks on autopilot and then I'm placing my pick-six; a hundred fifty dollars on the first place finisher in each of six consecutive races. No holds barred today. There only needs to be one good long shot in a pick-six to make the bet golden, but I luck out with two. As long as I haven't lost my touch, as long as my one-fifty doesn't tip anyone off, I should walk away with just shy of eighteen grand.

Then David's voice rattles inside my head about "this kid with headphones" who makes a killing around the tracks and I stuff them into my backpack. Even without music it's loud and the crowd feels good, electric. The last week of live racing is always a big turnout, cold snap or not.

I find a good seat out of the way and revel in the knowledge that I have a zero-percent chance of running into the Joshes here. I've only been aware of Asbury Bible College for a week but I'm already feeling a little claustrophobic. Twelve hundred students, that's it, so you start running into the same people in no time. My high school was bigger than that. Except for the recent cold spell the place feels more like a summer camp than a university. The activities, the all-night worship singalongs; campfires and acoustic guitars and s'mores.

But at the tracks there's a different sort of energy running through the crowd. You don't see it in people's faces—most look tired and cold today—but you feel it. Even the regulars I recognize, I know they're not going to be bugging me to get together and jam sometime. In an ocean of people I don't know I feel at home and I'm not sure what that means or if I care. Because here is another place I belong. Perfectly anonymous, perfectly at home.

After a while, a sign advertising dollar foot-long hot dogs

catches my eye. I pat for my wallet and head toward the stand. Two should be enough, and a large caffeinated drink. I know better than to risk the coffee. The two women behind the counter look me over like they're sizing me up.

"What? You think I can't finish t-two of these?" Motherfuck it with the stutter already.

The older of the two runs the back of her rubber-gloved wrist against her forehead and grunts a laugh, looking at the younger. A mother-daughter team, from the similarity in their eyes, noses, and sneery smiles. The daughter leans over and forces her thoughts through a thick Russian accent.

"Almost didn't recognize you, without the, what is," she points to her ears, "music. You know. Big music."

Dumbstruck and rapidly feeling nauseous I take the dogs and walk directly past the condiments, past the seat where I thought I wasn't being noticed and I keep walking through the doors to the outdoor seating area. The sun is bright in the cold blue sky and my shadow is stark on the pavement. Half blind I stumble over windblown trash and make my way to the far end of open seating. But where I expect to find plenty of room to sit and think there's a throng of race fans. Right. The last week of live racing. It's packed.

I spot an unoccupied table with a few trays and various leftovers, a spilled soda, whatever, sit down and clear a spot, try to wrap my head around the idea that I'm so well known even the food vendors recognize me.

With headphones on, the world's not really there. It makes it easier not to notice people noticing you, which was the entire reason I'd adopted my first set in middle school. Back then my stutter was still pretty bad and I was going to school with the same kids who'd watched me convulse and soil myself every other day. That's not something you get to leave behind without moving to Alaska. The best way to get through the day, any day, was to tune it all out and listen to heavy metal or punk rock.

I've been betrayed by my own coping mechanism.

Sweating in the cold, feeling a hundred thousand greedy eyes waiting for me to make my next move – who will it be? If I've learned anything it's that most people will take advantage of a good financial opportunity when it comes their way.

Raw paranoia explodes behind my eyes and I can feel the heaves before I have a chance to find a trashcan. I lean forward and burst open like a fire hydrant. Thank God there's no one in front of me, 'cause regardless of how empty my stomach felt moments ago I have no problem making quite a mess. Just before a second round of vomit, as the first pile is beginning to harden and freeze, my cell phone buzzes in my pocket. By the time I'm done people are really starting to notice. I dart for the exit, leaving the hot dogs for the crows.

After that, all I remember is feeling a pair of huge, powerful arms, an everlasting moment of total, weightless silence, then blackout.

I believe I can see the future
'Cause I repeat the same routine

PART II

I think I used to have a purpose
Then again, that might have been a dream

14:

No dreams.

I stir at the sound of a coffee maker kicking on, reach up for the light but nothing's there, pray that when my eyes adjust I'll be in my own place but the brightness of the room tells me it's larger than my entire apartment, though that isn't saying much.

Unable to get up, I take a quick note of my surroundings. Dusty planks of sunlight slice through the open space of the room. Venetian blinds. I smell coffee and leather, old books, some kind of stale smoke, not cigarettes, maybe sweeter cigars or pipe tobacco.

I'm warm, lying on some type of long couch that sticks to my skin. Leather. Vinyl. My head is heavy with hunger and I shake for lack of caffeine. If I wasn't feeling so sick, I could feasibly get up and walk out, which brings on an acute sense of desperation.

A man's voice from the dark side of the room, behind me.

"I see you're awake."

I know the voice from somewhere a long time ago. I'm waiting for the glint of a high nickel steel blade of some bizarrely imagined fantasy knife, or maybe the sound of a handgun being cocked; all to make my fear a little more real. Nothing.

My lips are caked together with old vomit. I begin to heave at the taste, but instead my throat closes down hard and I choke on a collection of mucus. I spit on the floor in an act of opportunistic defiance, then immediately regret it, unsure how my kidnapper might react. When nothing happens I almost whimper.

"I've been watching you for some time, Ezekiel."

Like a good captive I finally ask, "Where am I?"

"You're safe. I'm here to help."

"Help?"

"Like you helped me."

It can't be.

"How are you...alive?"

"You do remember."

"Let's get this over—"

"Relax. You were in pretty bad shape out there. This isn't what it seems."

"Well it seems like you've k-kidnapped me."

"We can work through the details later. Try to eat something."

A burst of light from another set of blinds brings the room into better focus. Next to me is a table with a sandwich and a large plastic cup, dripping with condensation. I reach for it.

"I have a pot of normal coffee brewing as well, so you can have your choice. Or both." A pause. "I'm locking this door for now. It's not that I don't trust you, or...it's...you probably don't trust me yet."

"Never did."

He crosses the room but due to the angle of the light I can only see a pair of pleated khaki pants, two hands, and a bag, my bag, which he sets down near the couch.

"I'm happy to see you kept up with your writing. You have no idea how important these are."

The door closes and the room falls silent enough to hear all the little things that happen when a house is cold but the sun is shining bright. I sit up and take stock of the room, looking for a way out. The door is solid oak. Looking out the window, it must be at least five stories up. An apartment. I don't recognize any streets or buildings, can't quite make out the—

"Books."

Holy shit. The dark side of the room has come into focus. Ten plus feet of floor-to-ceiling shelves surround me on three sides. Their spines encroach and retreat, shake as if it were an earthquake, playing off both my hunger and paranoia. The room spins, then stops, or maybe I fell, I don't remember.

I do remember sucking down the iced coffee and begging it to kick in. Within three and a half minutes of pacing the room I'm fairly certain there's nothing to do but wait. There aren't any bookends or blunt objects in sight so I pocket a metal pen, in case things get desperate.

When the door opens again I'm sitting back on the leather couch, a psychologist's couch, brain still rattled, aware of the pen in my left pocket just out of sight. He starts talking as if no time had passed.

"So, Ezekiel, were you really planning a prank for the last day of school, or did you just get lucky?"

"What do you think?"

"What I think doesn't matter."

"Well it certainly had an impact on my life."

"I'm not here to argue."

"I spent almost an entire school year sitting in a utility closet and you signed off on it."

He sighs. "I was fresh out of grad school."

"Yeah, well fast forward to about an hour ago. I thought you were dead."

He sighs almost theatrically. "I guess I was, once."

"Cut the theatrics. You know what I mean."

"But you don't know what I mean."

"Why should I give a steaming shit what you mean?"

He waits a moment, then says, "You remember what you told me, the day before Mrs. Fiore died?"

I don't even bother to nod.

"Well, my daughter was still in middle school when I started meeting with you. You have to understand how it sounded, like you were just playing games. Making things up. She didn't have any high-school friends.

"But a few years after you got me... Long after I was fired, when she was a sophomore, one of her older cheerleader friends made a pass at me and..." another sigh, "...you were right. I really wanted her. Only to touch her." I turn around and he's looking right at me but his eyes are miles away. For a moment the tables are turned. I feel more like the therapist than the patient.

"But you didn't?"

"No, I let my wife drive her home. When they were gone, I could've shot myself. Like that." He snaps his fingers and I jump. "I'd felt the smallest tinge of lust for a girl half my age and if you hadn't said what you did those years before...I might have given in. Stephanie and I had been having problems for years. This girl was so young and perfect, so willing. But I couldn't get your voice out of my head. Tragedy...you said."

"She was tall and blonde, with a white and blue uniform. Hoop earrings, awkward bangs."

Something between a sigh and a laugh cuts the tension in the room. "I...still don't believe it."

"You'd have died in a car accident. Probably that night."

He doesn't say anything.

"Look, I don't mean to be insensitive...I mean, this is all great, but Mona isn't here right?"

"Who?"

"Good. So let's cut to the chase. You've been following me. You've been calling. Now I'm here and I don't know how, so—"

I hear something in the background, a hushed, almost scratching sound.

"Are you actually taking notes this time?"

"I'm trying not to repeat past mistakes, Ezekiel. You said her name was Mona?"

"So this is your first kidnapping?"

"I was trying to keep you safe."

He ends his last entry with a period, *pip*.

A moment.

"When your teacher died, as much as I wanted to chalk that up to coincidence I couldn't shake the thought... But then I discussed it with one of my professors and he had me convinced that you were more than likely having trouble dealing with the loss of your mom."

"Step-mom."

"When I had that close call with the cheerleader it was your voice I heard. It was your words that kept me from giving in. After that I couldn't stop thinking about you. I wanted to figure you out, but all I've had to go on was my memory because, as you've pointed out, I wasn't taking so many notes back then.

"I made mistakes and I'm sorry."

"There were a lot of mistakes made."

He sits forward, saying, "Do you remember our sessions that summer? When we did those relaxation exercises."

"Not really. It's been a while since I thought about you at all." This seems to hit deep, so I shrug, almost apologize.

"We did regressive hypnosis. We walked through some of your dreams. I thought you were faking, that you were...a very good storyteller. It seemed like you were creating a fantasy world as an escape, like my colleague had suggested. And of course, the trauma of seeing your teacher get shot."

"I killed her, you know."

The sound of his pen stops.

"I knew about that stray bullet. I put her in its path and you know it."

"I don't know it so much as I'm baffled by it."

I sit up a little. "I suppose I should apologize, too." I'd basically accused him of touching me, the bad way. To get him fired.

"You know that's always made me wonder. If that hadn't happened, would my wife and I have had so much trouble in the first place?"

"Come again?"

"She left me for a few months after losing my job, because of the allegations. Took Stacy, our daughter, off to her mother's. Then we...resolved things, settled back in, but—"

"It was never the same, huh?"

"Nope."

"Shit, man. Sorry." I'm still feeling that cold metal pen in my pocket.

"And I know it's sort of a chicken and egg question now, but I wonder if things would have followed that same path, even without, you know..."

"Me getting you canned. Right."

"Anyway, I don't blame you. I brought it on myself in a way." He almost laughs. "I should have been the one person you could trust, but all I knew to do was suggest medication for someone who displayed your...characteristics."

"Luckily Dad couldn't afford the drugs."

"Hmmm."

"Don't laugh, but did you know he was a multi-millionaire at one point?"

"Didn't you and Edward do the meal program? Food stamps and...I don't mean to be rude, but your clothes and everything."

"No, you're right. That was how we lived. See, my dad inherited all this money when his dad died, he was nineteen or twenty, I think, and anyway, he spent most of it before I was born. Now he sits around in a house he bought back in the seventies, the only one he has left. It's paid for, but it's falling apart because he doesn't have the money to fix it up. He never learned anything but how to spend money and now he's too afraid to go out in the real world at all."

"Agoraphobia?"

"Not quite. He sees every time he leaves the house as another chance to get in a car accident or spill coffee on someone and get sued. He's afraid of losing what little money he has left. And the less he spends on the house, the longer he'll last until going broke."

"Interesting."

"To you, maybe. To me it meant having an unemployed, paranoid loser for a role model."

"So what does he live on?"

"The way my aunt tells it, when I was about a year old, he stuck his remaining wealth into a savings account hoping the interest might add another few years to his 'financial longevity'. He's too paranoid to invest and risk losing anything." Jesus, I'm talkative all of the sudden. "Course, he doesn't talk about this stuff. But yeah, one generation was a serious risk-taker, investor, entrepreneur—Grandpa even held a few patents—and the next generation is a huddled ball of insecurity."

He turns a page on his yellow legal pad and gives that last thought some breathing room.

"Why don't we talk about you now?"

"Fine," I sigh. Shit, my guard is down, when did that happen? Instinctively I reach for the pen, remembering why I swiped it. Something still feels off.

"And please, call me Heath."

"We'll see... Mr. Fucking Jepson. Unbelievable."

A moment.

"Okay. Tell me about Ethan Johnson."

"Who?"

"Remember? The big playground equipment lawsuit."

"Ethan..."

He waits for me to go on, but I don't, so he subtly clears his throat.

"Oh, right. It's just...I never knew his name."

We covered a lot that afternoon. His notion is that since I was obviously able to alter the future by causing my teacher to walk into the path of a bullet, and that he'd changed his own future by choosing not to fool around with that girl, that maybe there was something about my end-of-life vision that was a key for me to unlock. He even remembers me talking about having coffee with a girl in a library and then the chaos that would ensue before it all went out of focus. It was the coffee part that caught his attention, since my father didn't drink it and I was only nine.

I look at the clock.

"Sorry to cut this short, but...I'm meeting her around sunset."

"Mona?"

"Yeah."

"A date?"

"If you want to call it that."

"So I assume she's not aware of this meeting."

"Nope, but I've seen it a hundred times. It's going to happen."

"You know she's the key, don't you?"

"I hope so."

He hands me a business card on which he'd already circled his number in red ink, the number I'd rejected so many times the past few days.

"It says Office but it's my cell phone. In case anything comes up. Don't worry, we'll figure this out."

"Easy for you to say."

"I guess so. Then again, I'm sitting here aren't I? Still breathing."

"So, can we swing by the tracks? I need to cash out."

"Big winner?"

"You wouldn't believe."

From the moment we stepped out of his apartment, I don't think we spoke, or even communicated, beyond a few simple nods. I did manage to slip the pen from one pocket to the other, to keep it out of his sight. If I didn't need to stab him in the throat, I could always return it later.

I was in and out of Canterbury in ten minutes.

"Well, my car is around the side there." I can't think of anything else to say. 'See you around' sounds too familiar, and will I? Honestly, I don't know. He'd been flying below the radar thus far, who knows where this would lead? Instead, I spin on my heels before the awkward silence compels me to puke out some pleasantry like, 'Take it easy' or 'Have a nice night'.

"Zeek."

I stop.

"Don't worry."
I walk on.

15:

Elliot Park is a rendezvous point for murders of crows every fall because it has some of the oldest trees within the city limits, several easily a hundred feet tall. With the sudden cold this year the leaves are falling before they've had a chance to change color and now trees are fully clothed in black. The crows' mournful cries resonate hollow and cold against old brick buildings as the icy wind carries their melancholy symphony down shadowed alleys.

Like walking right into a cliché, a misty fog lurches in off the river, veiling the city, diffusing the stronger lights and devouring the weaker ones. The mist seeps in between the teeth of my jacket's zipper, creeps up around my ankles, bleeding upward and inward. The only thing missing is a full moon shining down on a lone serial killer, walking blade in hand down the middle of the road.

Thoughts of Mona alone sustain me but she's late and my confidence is waning. I catch myself humming "Ain't No Sunshine When She's Gone", playing it off when the occasional student walks by. Number One passes, leading a pack of guitar playing buddies toward a big fat Lincoln that just screams televangelist. I try to avoid eye contact and fail.

"Hey, man, we're heading to this open mic in the Warehouse District. It's like, a coffee shop and a church at the same time. Corner Coffee, I think. You want to come along?"

"No thanks."

"You already stood me up once, man. You won't be able to avoid me forever."

"I can try."

A pause. "What?"

"Nothing, man. You have fun at your 'jam session' tonight." I make air-quotes for effect.

"You sound a little bitter, man. Do you need someone to talk to?"

Maybe he was half joking, but still, I flip him the bird. I decide he's worse than Eddie because he's actually got a talent to waste. Mastering Coltrane's "Giant Steps" is no walk in the park. I've never even tried, and he seemed to pull it off without any effort.

He closes the guitars inside the oversized trunk while his buddies climb in then he lumbers over, drops his voice like a good camp counselor about to confront the unruly child. Hand on shoulder. Face marking concern, empathy, right on cue.

"Look, Zeek, you'd probably make more friends out here if you tried a little harder?"

"I'm not here to make friends."

He shakes his head, saying, "Why are you so hostile?"

"Why are you so persistent? It's like you don't even realize no one likes you. You think those guys would be your friends if you didn't have connections. Or a car? You're a means to an end, man."

That must have hit a chord. He turns without a word.

"But hey, don't be bitter. I'll be here if you need someone to talk to." He's already slamming the door. The brake lights set the fog on this half of the block ablaze, then slink around the corner and disappear.

Alone again. Standing near the parking lot entrance of Miller Hall for over two hours, freezing, trying to act like I'm waiting for a ride. Mona never comes through those doors.

Something is broken. Maybe if I hadn't helped Eddie out last summer he'd never have learned to rely on me in the first place. He never would've called me for a place to stay because he'd still be leeching off Dad. Then Sunday afternoon Mona and I would have met like we were supposed to and right now I'd be walking with her and getting to know her and things would be perfect. It's also hard to shake what Heath said, that Mona is the key, which only serves to reinforce the sense of urgency tugging at my gag reflex.

I give up and head over to Gallagher's, waiting for the neon to pierce the fog but the signs aren't on at all. I see lights in the apartments upstairs, so it's not an outtage. The place is dead.

"Zeek?" A girl's voice out of the darkness, but with the wind it's hard to tell from which direction.

"Mona?"

Then I distinguish a thin outline that resembles Shelley coming to meet me out of the park.

"Who?"

"Shelley. Hi. Lovely night for an ear infection, wouldn't you say?"

"What's going on? I'm supposed to work till close tonight. Place is all locked up. I mean, with a chain between the door handles and everything. What in the heck?"

"Have you called D-David?"

"Yeah, I got his voicemail, but I didn't leave a message. Well, you know."

"Yeah, he hates voicemail. Well, I'm going to guess you've got the night off. I'll give him a call, see if I can get through, figure this out."

I touch her shoulder, tell myself I'm being reassuring.

"Okay."

"Don't worry. I'm sure there's a good explanation."

She looks around like she's about to say something but the wind picks up, provoking a fervor of caws and screeches from the trees so loud you can't even hear the wind for a moment.

"Well, it looks like I'm free until midnight. If you want to do something?"

"Or what, you'll turn into a pumpkin?"

She shrugs.

"Well, that's a little early for me, but I suppose. Can I buy you a drink?"

"It's sort of late for coffee."

"I was thinking more like... Oh, but you don't, do you?"

She shakes her head.

"I guess we could get a sandwich somewhere."

She drops her head, probably blushing but there's not enough light to tell. Of all people, Shelley?

"I'm sorry. I should go." She scurries back across the street, stops at the corner. I wait to see her disappear into the fog, but she stands there. The bus stop sign glints under the dim streetlight as it shakes in another gust of wind. I walk up next to her.

"Why d-don't I wait here with you? Nothing better to do."

"Aren't you cold?"

"I went numb hours ago."

"Well, thanks." She looks down to her feet. I think she's smiling. I would've come up with something more to say, but the bus rounds the corner before anything comes to mind.

"This is me."

The brakes squeal to a halt and send a frantic mass of crows into the air. I'm about to say goodnight when Eddie comes barreling out of the bus and grabs me by my coat collar with his hand, shoving me up against a tree, and socks me with his stump.

"What the Hell, man? Why didn't you tell me your boss lives in Wisconsin?"

"Well, you n-never asked, for starters. Get off me." I straighten my jacket. "And actually, I had no idea. What d-does that have to do with anything?"

"It makes a huge difference when you're trying to, oh, I don't know, repossess a fucking car."

The bus pulls away but both Shelley and Eddie's eyes are glued to my face.

"What is he talking about?"

Eddie just stares so it's up to me.

"Let's get inside."

* * *

The walk to my place doesn't take nearly long enough. I pull the light on and realize I haven't had much company.

"Sorry for the mess. Eddie just moved in and we're, you know..."

"What do you mean? This is pretty much what it looked like when I got here."

"Thanks, Eddie."

"Oh."

He takes the couch and Shelley reluctantly settles in to the beanbag chair in the corner. She gives the air a couple sniffs, then decides to stand.

"Let me bring you up to speed. Eddie works in collections, and through a complicated series of events I still don't fully understand, I only found out this morning that D-d- ah...our boss, that is, is in a bit of financial trouble. You know all those cars he has?" She nods. "Well, it seems many of them are in the red."

"That's what I do," Eddie jumps in, grinning like an idiot. "I collect on car loans and when needed, repossess them. Only the process is different when they're registered in Wisconsin."

"And you didn't notice this when you saw the plates?"

"They're custom plates."

"So?"

"So, no."

"So, you're an idiot."

"Fuck you." He whacks me in the chest with his stump and Shelley stares wide-eyed just long enough for Eddie to notice.

"Oh this?" He waves it around, "Yeah, I've been thinking about getting one of those hooks or something. Wouldn't that be sweet?"

"Eddie, please."

"I'm only saying; pirates are cooler than ninjas."

"You only say that because you sucked as a one-handed ninja."

"To-*may*-to, to-*mah*-to."

Shelley cuts in. "Boys. Seriously. Can we get back to the topic at hand?"

I nod in approval. "Well played."

"What?" Shelley looks at me quizzically. Then she gets it, laughing despite herself. Eddie looks confused.

Shelley leans forward, saying, "Look. Mr. Ezekiel's Annoying Little Brother, I'm about—"

"Half-brother."

"Whatever. All I want to know is: What's going on with Gallagher's?"

"Right, okay." He rubs his face. "So, for most states, I would send the right letters and when they expire, thirty days or so, I can repo the car. Do it all day every day.

"On David's accounts, all his mail goes to his office here in Minneapolis. Some office he rents downtown near that jewelry store he co-owns with some Jewish guy."

Shelley cuts in. "Easy on the Anti-Semitism."

"Sorry. La Hymen. Anyway. Apparently he actually lives, as in, place of residence, about forty minutes from here, right across the border in Wisconsin. It only makes sense that all his cars are registered in Wisconsin to his home address.

"In my job, I can't even say the word 'repossess' to a Wisconsin resident without getting in trouble. They have totally different laws. It's one of the worst states."

"Cut to the chase, Eddie."

"If you want to take a car in Wisconsin, it's called a replevin. It's an expensive legal process and it takes a long time. Since we've been sending all the wrong letters for months now, legally we have to start over, to send the right letters and wait at least thirty days before we can start filing the court paperwork. We also have to cross our fingers that he isn't aware of how many laws we broke in the first place. So basically, I won't be getting a bonus this month, just like I haven't for the past few, apparently all because of your boss."

Shelley cuts in. "From the looks of things, we're not going to get paid at all so I think you're complaining to the wrong people."

"Look, let's relax, okay." I try to mediate but it backfires.

"Who are you to tell me to relax? You lied to me out there like you didn't know what was going on."

"Sorry. Really, I am."

"You're sorry, he's sorry. We're still out of a job."

I let Shelley blow off some steam for a moment, then turn back to Eddie. "Where do we stand?"

"All the small business stuff is handled somewhere else, but I spoke with them and it looks like they've been ready to drop the hammer for a while now. I had no idea. All his business accounts are under a Tax ID, not his social-security number. When the different collection groups got together this morning and compared balances, well, the shop and the jewelry store were the most solvent."

The cold wind outside whips frozen grass and weeds against the ice covered window panes.

"Well, anybody want coffee? I know I need some."

"No way," Eddie stretches, yawning, "I have to get up super early tomorrow. We do Saturdays once a month."

I step into the kitchen and find a fresh layer of broken glass covering the counter and sink, leaving only a plastic handle.

"Eddie, what the Hell?"

"What the Hell what? I have to work in—"

I hold up the handle. "The coffee pot."

"I already told you, it was a cooking accident."

"No, I mean the one I just bought. After the cooking accident." I throw the handle at his back. "The new one I just dropped sixty bucks on."

"Oh yeah, right. Holy shit! Holy shit, man! That one tried to kill me!" He's practically bouncing off the couch.

"Are you going completely stupid on me?"

"I'm serious! It exploded right in my hand. I could've died!"

I bury my face in my hands. "Go on."

"I was gonna do some dishes this morning, after you left, to try and help out since I'm not paying you any rent."

"I don't remember agreeing to that."

"Hmm... Anyway, when I rinsed out the coffee pot it blew up in my hand."

Shelley and I look right at each other and in unison we say, "Cold water."

"Huh?"

"He's your brother, you tell him."

I rub my temples. "When something is very hot, and made of glass, it is very sensitive to sudden changes in temperature. Kind of like when you drop an ice cube in a glass of hot tea..."

He stares.

"...It cracks. This is fifth-grade science."

"Whoopty-doo. Science. What does that have to do with your coffee pot?"

"So when you run a piping hot coffee pot under ice-cold Minnesota tap water, it explodes."

"You don't have to say it all sarcastic, jeeze. Sorry, okay?"

"Don't worry about it. I think it has a warranty. You could have at least swept up the glass."

I stare into the pile of debris and David comes to mind, losing his business today, only a month from losing many of his cars; I wonder how much more before he cracks.

"Wait a minute. Topic at hand? No hand," Eddie waves his stump, "I get it. Classic."

"Holy shit, Eddie. Are you serious?"

"He's your brother."

Shelley decides to go wait for the next bus. Eddie goes to bed.

I dump the coffee-pot remains into the trash and find half a dozen empty cups inside. It looks like Eddie has been hitting the iced coffee pretty hard.

I look forward to falling asleep that night, 'cause even if Mona didn't show up earlier, I could always count on her to be in my dreams.

16:

No dreams. Right. How could I forget?

It makes me wonder if I've outlived my final dream. When Eddie screwed up my meeting with Mona last Sunday, did that throw a wrench in the works and change things enough that I'm now living in the real, bona fide future? Is this what survival feels like?

I decide to seek a little guidance from the only other person I know who is still alive and definitely shouldn't be. He answers after two rings.

"Mr. Jepson?" I still can't call him by his first name.

"Morning, Ezekiel."

"Look, I have some things I need to get off my chest. Think we could get together?" I twirl the silver pen between my fingers and thumb.

"Okay, sure." He yawns. "Sorry. Fell asleep a little while ago."

"Long night?"

"I work security. Third shift. It doesn't pay as well as therapy, but they have good benefits."

I don't know what to say. That's pretty much my fault, one way or another. The silence hangs like a stone until he speaks up.

"I'm...past it."

A pause.

"When is a good time to meet?" I ask.

"Three or four, probably."

"Let's make it four, then."

"Alright, should we meet at Gallagher's?"

"Coffee sounds good," then I remember, "but the shop is closed."

"Really? Some holiday I missed?"

"Nope. Lock and chain closed. Long story. I'll think of a place."

"See you at four."

With Eddie probably on his bus to work, no doubt ruining someone else's life today, I have the apartment to myself. I'm out of food, so I grab my coat and head over to Hell's Kitchen.

Over an incredible plate of Bison Benedict smothered in tangerine-jalapeno hollandaise I try not to ponder my dilemma any further. I try to enjoy the food and the admittedly good coffee, but it's not enough of a distraction.

No single thought stands out in my head. They're all screaming around at once. I catch myself bobbing my knee up and down making the chair squeak.

"Bet you won't be needing that coat later." The waiter shocks me out of my stupor.

"You know something I don't?"

"Indian summer."

"What?"

"Watch the news once in a while. It's supposed to be in the mid-sixties today. Clear and sunny. A nice break from that little cold spell."

He drops the check and sidles up to his next table, makes a similar comment about how overdressed they are. I pay the bill. It's already warming up so I toss my jacket over my arm and walk home with new eyes. At any moment something else could happen and catch me completely off guard. I'm not sure I like it. The only thing I can be sure of right now is that on a day like this Mona should be reading outside. It's the closest thing I have to a guarantee and I'll take it.

* * *

"How was Arizona?" She jumps and almost drops her book, caught a little off guard since I approached from behind the tree.

"Hi. Sheesh."

"Well...?"

"Well," she pauses, smiling, "It was about eighty degrees warmer than it was here, but today's shaping up to be nice."

I can feel a stutter coming on so I simply nod.

"Yeah, I got stuck in Denver yesterday, quite a storm, so I caught the red eye this morning."

I nod again. That wasn't supposd to happen, either. It was supposed to be our night last night. Didn't someone say something once about a butterfly flapping its wings in Peking, and it caused a tornado, or something? I can't remember, but I spend a little too long trying to think of it.

"So..." She blushes, a little confused at my silence.

"Glad you made it b-back safe."

She nods. "By the way, what happened to the shop?"

"Closed, I guess. So what are you reading?"

"Oh, uh, Inferno. It's for a lit class." Her face is distracted, "I'm sorry, but the place up and closed in what, three days?"

"Yeah."

"Hmm." She furrows her eyebrows.

"What?"

"You seem to be perfectly fine with it. Not a care in the world from the looks of you."

"I save what I can." Instinctively, I reach for the cashier's check in my pocket and make a mental note to get to the bank.

"I don't know. I'd be going nuts if I lost my job just like that."

I sit on the bench next to her tree and she gets up to sit next to me. She's waiting for some kind of pleasant reply. I want to tell her how I'm more stressed than she could imagine; how employment is the least of my concerns. What would a normal person say?

"I probably should be more worried than I am."

"No, no... You've got the right attitude. Worrying doesn't get you anywhere."

"We should do something later. I know a few places around with halfway decent coffee. If you're interested."

She runs her fingers along the cover of her book, thinking it over.

For some reason just now I'm struck with the realization that she doesn't wear any makeup at all. Her eyelashes are naturally dark, she has a normal complexion, not perfect, but what do I care? The freckles here and there are cute.

Most girls at this school seem to be relishing their first moments out from under their parents' watchful eyes; blue eyeshadow, push-up bras, fake nails and three cans of hairspray a night and bam, they all look like televangelists' wives.

But Mona, she has this simple beauty, and a confidence I can't help but envy.

"I think I can adjust my schedule."

"Good."

"And while we're at it, why don't you show me around? This city has changed a lot since I lived here."

"You lived here?" There's some new information.

"A long time ago. I hardly remember." Her eyes grow distant, nostalgic for a moment.

"I'd love to."

"What time?"

"How does five sound?"

"Fine with me. Let's meet here..." she takes my hand and writes her four-digit dorm room extension in red ink. "...and don't be late. If you're running behind, call. I hate to be kept waiting for a date." She reads my face. "Don't worry, we can go Dutch. Now if you'll excuse me, I have to meet someone for breakfast."

"A breakfast date, too?" My voice might have cracked.

She seems pleased at the hint of jealousy.

"I'm meeting up with the new roommate, trying to find a reason not to hate her annoying guts. One of that Joshua guy's fans. You know the type."

"The ring-by-spring crowd."

"Exactly. Now all you need to do is pray that my lunch date doesn't wear me out."

"You're joking."

"Am I? See you at five."

* * *

I buy some batteries at the corner store and fire up the MP3 player—remember, this is 2006—and then walk around downtown scoping out the other coffee joints. The truth is I'd never checked out the competition after starting at Gallagher's. I try a few too many, sure, but I want to make sure I find the best. By four o'clock I'm physically exhausted but still heavily caffeinated.

"So, I've been dying to know; how much was that ticket for yesterday?"

"Enough that they didn't want to hand me cash. Anyway, that might all be over now."

I find an empty picnic table and we sit.

"What do you mean?"

"That's what I wanted to talk about. I didn't dream last night. Haven't for a few nights, actually. First time this has happened in over nine years. I close my eyes and nothing happens and then I wake up."

"Hmm."

"Things have been really off track. Little things are adding up, everything is blurring together. The days, I mean. Then Mona wasn't even there last night. I stood around for two hours."

"Really?"

"Yeah. She ended up taking a flight this morning from Arizona, weather delays somewhere else, butterfly effect kind of shit... I mean, how am I supposed to figure this thing out now? Fuckin' Eddie."

"Eddie? Your brother?"

I'm digging at someone's initials carved into the aging wood of the tabletop.

"I was helping him out Sunday when Mona and I were supposed to meet. I completely forgot, and since then everything has been off. Or maybe it was before that. I don't even know what started it. Now I don't know what to expect next."

"Like the rest of us, you mean." He laughs in a way that makes me uneasy. "You know, I'm struck by something. Do you even realize how...self-absorbed you are?"

"Self-absorbed?"

"Every statement you make eventually comes back to how things are going to affect you. You're so worried about saving your own skin, I wonder, do you even care about this girl?"

I stand up, face pulsing, teeth clenched, saying, "Listen. I'm messed up in ways you can't even begin to grasp. I don't have time to worry about other people."

"Hey, easy. I half agree with you. Sit down. Relax."

I look around but no one seems to have noticed.

"Think about this: Over the years you've had all that knowledge, prior knowledge, and... Has it ever crossed your mind that Mona may not be the key to your life? What if you're the key to hers? If that last dream really is the end, if you're really going to die, then don't you think she's going to die right there with you?"

He waits for that one to sink in then lowers his voice to a near whisper.

"If I were you, I'd be trying to figure out a way to save her."

"Look, you have some good points, and yeah, it's not like I never considered that." A lie. "But that doesn't make me self-absorbed."

"I'm only saying this because I'm trying to help. I don't think you're some kind of self-centered asshole. Obviously you care about your brother, letting him move in with you and all. And Mona, too. You've spent a lot of time getting to know her, so to speak.

"You've got a gift, but unless there are things you're not telling me, what good has come of it other than a few bucks off horse racing?"

"I've made more than a few bucks." I made damn good money, actually, but it feels stupid and shallow the moment the words come out.

"That's not the point. I'm sure going through all of those..." He scratches his stubbled chin. "...All those episodes. I'm sure that's taken an incredible toll. I can't even begin to imagine what it's been like so I won't sit here and act like I understand. I don't. I don't know how anyone could. But over the last few years, what have you done for anyone else? And I mean besides out of a feeling of obligation to your brother."

"Step-brother."

"Have you ever considered helping your father out with money? Have you ever considered trying to mentor Eddie in the areas where your father obviously failed the both of you? Or have you just been floating along, watching life pass you by?"

"Well none of that really matters now, d-does it? First off, I can't change the past. Second, things aren't happening the way I expect anymore anyway. Third, I didn't dream anything last night, so this so-called gift appears to be gone."

The setting sun throws our shadows long and thin across the grass. I watch them grow as we wait in silence. I buckle first.

"Sorry about all that."

"Don't be. I don't blame you. This is a lot of shit to go through."

I chuckle. "You can say 'shit'?"

"Of course I can say 'shit'. I'm a security guard now. It's practically in the job description."

I laugh and the tension dissolves a little more.

"Oh yeah. Right below the dress code. The mandatory swearing. How could I forget?"

"Look, I'll see you around."

Heath gets into his Oldsmobile and rolls down the window.

"You should get going," he says, looking at his wrist.

"I suppose all I have to do is avoid libraries, right?"

He shakes his head. "When the time comes, and I think you'll recognize it, you have to go right into that library and get Mona out."

17:

I've got the big, beautiful unknown stretched out before me like a giant theater curtain, constantly revealing no more than one moment at a time. What you might think of as a normal day. I also have a real date with Mona to look forward to, the kind of date where anything can happen in real time.

I head home to change into something nice, which means the same khakis I wore the other day and any shirt that's still on a hanger. Pull the light off on my way back out. Eddie's smoking on the back porch again and I steal the thing right from his hand and take a drag to see if that might calm me down. I nearly choke and Eddie laughs. Screw him. I'm flirting with death enough as it is.

Making my way back over to Elliot Park I see Mona's waiting, reading. The clock on my cell phone says I'm right on time.

She hears me approach and without looking up she says, "Ready to go?"

"Ready when you are."

But then she sits for a moment with her eyes fixed just below my face.

"Are you staring at my chest?"

"No," she almost blushes. "I'm admiring your crucifix. It's very ornate."

"There's a story behind that."

"Indulge me."

"First, we walk. I need to decide if you're someone I can share my secrets with." This conversation, it's different. I'm shooting from the hip, living in the moment.

"Okay, I'm intrigued." She stands, brushing the leaves and grass away from her legs. "Where are we off to?"

I haven't decided. Since anything can happen right now I simply turn and start walking. A moment later she loops her arm through my elbow and we carry on in silence heading somewhat north and east (Minneapolis streets line up with the river so they don't run along any of the cardinal directions).

Everything about being with her is energizing. The weight of her arm around mine, the glimmer of chance in her eyes, the way her hair moves freely in the wind. She floats along through each motion like a feather on the wind. Every little thing she does reminds me it's her decision to be with me in this moment of real, tangible time. She could be doing anything at all in the world but she's chosen to spend time with me. I feel bold.

We're moving toward the river and I think, it's nice to be with someone who doesn't feel the need to fill every moment with idle conversation. The echo of St. Anthony Falls envelops us, drowning out the sound of traffic as we pass the old Gold Medal Flour building. There's construction in progress next to a hotel but the equipment sits idle. There's always some crew reinforcing the old structures for the Mill City Museum or tearing down a hopeless lot to make room for new condos. We move closer to the river until the sound echoes all around like a chorus of ghosts.

"I remember this place." She speaks up as we stand above a deep, hollowed-out lot with bulldozers and blinking orange signs all around. Copper pipes stick up out of the ground in the middle like arteries of what used to be a giant mechanical heart. The sun is almost gone and the construction equipment casts long, insect-like shadows in the dirt.

"This is where I learned to dance. When I was seven, my father would take me ice-skating. Over on Washington," she points toward the rink. "But one time when we drove all the way out it was closed. So we went for a walk and ended up here. Where that hole is, there was a courtyard with plants and benches around the outside. Then you stepped down onto the landing where there were tables around a fountain. See those pipes... Small trees hung with white Christmas lights stood between the tables. Year round, if I remember right."

I imagine the trees must have glowed the way her eyes do now as she pauses in the memory. She puts her hands on her cheeks, sighs, then spins once around, arms akimbo, uninhibited. Reliving some cherished innocent moment.

"I stood on his feet and he taught me how to dance. Do you know how to dance? It's a very important thing."

"I never learned."

"Well that makes things difficult, because you're supposed to lead."

"I'll put that on my to-do list."

"Good, because I'm certainly not going to teach you. It wouldn't be right and I can't believe you would even suggest such a thing."

She furls her eyebrows as if she's sincerely upset with me for a moment, then laughs it off. She's in a very good mood and it's becoming clear to me that I have absolutely no idea what to do with a girl on a date. I only hope she doesn't pick up on that fact.

I take her by the arm, it's my only move at the moment, and we walk north.

What to do, what to do, what to— "There are some really incredible buildings downtown." Really? Buildings? What the Hell do I know about architecture? Does she even like that sort of—

"After you."

Here goes nothing. We approach the first building from the east, because this way most of it stays out of sight until you round the corner, then it's all you can see. It's fortunate that the north and west sides of the building have no close neighbors, otherwise it would be difficult to appreciate its breathtaking scale.

All I can think to say in the moment is, "This is the ING building."

It's like a contemporary version of the Parthenon; over a hundred feet tall with white, modernly tapered columns that reach down from a flat roof, growing more and more narrow until they meet the ground. The north side of the building is the entrance, and the roof and columns extend beyond the main building fifty feet to create an enormous, open-air foyer. At least I think that's what it's called. The façade is glass and in between the columns covering the other three walls are huge slabs of green and white marble.

Her face says she's thinking something so I ask, "What?"

A moment.

"Nothing."

A moment.

"Nothing?"

"Well, don't laugh, okay. I see a face. In the rock."

She points to an area about ten feet around, divided in half by a seam in the marble. The pieces have been cut then laid open so they mirror each other.

"Pareidolia."

"Your what hurts?"

"It's kind of like a Rorschach thing. You know, the inkblots?"

"Okay."

"Well, that's not exactly right. Anyway, you're supposed to see things in the inkblots, right? Pareidolia is this psychological phenomenon where we readily recognize patterns in nature, in this case, a face, and then your brain gives it meaning."

"Well aren't you Encyclopedia Brown?"

"Har har. So when people see faces in naturally occurring things, like the man in the moon, that face on Mars, Jesus in an oak tree—"

"Oh, a real skeptic, are we?"

"—or when that woman in Florida saw the Virgin Mary in a grilled cheese sandwich."

"You're kidding, right?"

"Laugh it up, but that thing sold for twenty-eight grand on eBay. Too bad she took a bite out of it first, or it probably would have sold for more."

"You're not joking? A sandwich?"

"Hand on my heart."

"Unbelievable."

"Look, there's another face over there." I found a completely different pattern that held to the same basic elements necessary to constitute a human face. "There's nothing there but rock, you and I know that, but our minds will play tricks on us if we're not careful. See, a larger nose, squinty eyes, a bit of a sneer."

"Oh yeah, look at that..." She thinks for a moment. "Well, Mary or no Mary, I'd have still eaten the sandwich."

"No. That lady from Florida was brilliant. She had more vision than most. She didn't just see the Virgin Mary. She saw a way to cash in."

"So it's all about money?"

"For her, yeah. For the people with shrines to Jesus' crusty face on an old tailgate, no. To them, it's about a desire to get closer to God, I guess."

"Okay, I can see that."

"People visit those shrines from miles away sometimes, if they get enough news coverage."

She turns abruptly, putting herself right in front of me.

"Some people see Jesus and that's it. I saw a face in the marble. The grilled-cheese lady saw a way to make money. What do you see?"

I smile back.

"What?"

She waits.

I tilt my head without breaking eye contact, though it takes a lot of nerve. This elicits a second, more-drawn-out, "Wha-at?"

It's all I can do to smile and turn, taking her arm again. We zigzag around the city, finding other interesting architectural quirks. She notes things that are new or different and points out the older buildings she remembers from her early years.

We toss change into the fountain behind the big ugly government center that looks like a giant letter H, for Hennepin County, I guess, then head up 3rd Ave to 10th Street and press our hands against the vertical glass waterfall of an otherwise non-descript office building.

As the sun disappears the landscape changes from the harsh light of late afternoon to the shifting shadows and unnatural glow of mercury-vapor lights. We take a different route back to Elliot Park.

"We've got one more stop." We walk back over to where we met. She waits for me to do something, and I let her wait, a small confidence building inside me, happy that she hasn't lost interest yet.

"This is where we started, Ezekiel."

"See that bench?"

She nods quizzically.

"That's where I found Jesus."

"Oh, so you are a believer? I was having my doubts."

"The crucifix." I hold it up from my neck. "I found it under this bench when I was about eight years old. I grew up outside Saint Paul, but my step-mom helped out with little league back then." It was a chance for her to get out of the house, away from Dad's emotional black hole.

"One day there he was. Like most boys I was attracted to shiny objects. My step-mom helped me wash it off and put it on a chain for me."

"And let me guess, you've worn it ever since."

"Well, not exactly."

"Why not?"

"Now that's a long story."

"I've got time. Besides, that first story was okay, but it wasn't great."

"Well I'm sorry my childhood wasn't as quaint as yours."

"Oh, don't let my little dancing story fool you, it wasn't all peaches and cream. Finish the story."

"How about we say, to be continued?"

"When?"

"On our second date, of course."

"Aren't we confident?" She laughs. "Well, thanks for the walk. It's been...interesting and informative."

"Oh God. Was it really that bad?"

"It was nice. We'll have to do it again sometime."

"Fair enough. Now it's your t-turn."

"My turn?"

"Of course. You said we could go Dutch on this date. My idea was to go on an 'interesting and informative' walk down memory lane." I make air quotes in jest. "You're up."

"Well, I did say that, didn't I? Sharing stories doesn't count?"

"That all happened on my half."

She thinks for a moment and then an idea sparkles in her eyes. "Okay, meet me in TJ at seven."

"TJ?"

"You know – Miller, Carlson, TJ. The dorms."

I stare blankly.

"As in the T.J. Jones Memorial Library."

"You want t-t-to go to the library?" Back to stuttering in nothing flat.

"Of course not...but open dorms are at seven."

I'm not making the connection and I can't seem to push a single syllable out.

"The girls honor dorm is on the third floor, everyone calls it TJ to avoid sounding any more nerdy than we have to. As a boy, you can't come up to a girl's floor all alone, so I'll bring you up. At seven." She smiles as if everyone knows these things.

"You live in the l-library?" I try to keep a straight face. "I could d-die at any moment and-d-dy-dy-you live in the library?"

"Okay, what?" She backs up a step, but I feel myself begin to back away from her. I reach for a streetlamp to steady myself but the line begins to blur. My spine arches and it feels like the back of my head is going to reach the small of my back. I gasp for one last breath in freefall. Then everything grows uniformly distant and quiet and still.

* * *

I don't know how much time has passed but it's not quite silent. Mona sits across from me in a room with no books, staring deeply into her coffee like it's an oracle. There are many other people in the room, and it's the wrong kind of room. It's not our room. Not a single book in sight. She holds her coffee all wrong, for hours and hours, never letting go. It's in a paper cup with playing cards on the side, and I know it's not our coffee. No books. This is not our moment, not the one I've been dreaming since forever.

Oh God, is she mourning? Have I blown it?

Mourning. Mourning brings me back. If my brain is working I'm not dead. Am I asleep? Must be.

My mind slides back to a room filled with people, all in black, quiet. Mourners. Eddie is on his hands and knees, making his way through a forest of legs looking for me. He was small for his age back then, easily unnoticed. I'd found a good place to hide behind the communion altar and I could tell he was having a hard time finding me so I tossed a couple crackers when he was close enough to notice. He picked up the crackers and put them back on the altar, then slid next to me.

Eddie was hiding because his mother had just died and he didn't know what else to do. I decided to hide when Pastor Hildegard's brother showed up for the funeral.

The two men looked enough alike that my dad's eyes flared the instant he saw him, moving to intercept the man before he reached the church doors, fists clenched and resolute. Even as a nine-year-old I could guess it was a bad idea to show up for the funeral of your late brother's mistress. Especially when they burned to death in each other's arms. Poor little Bradon never had a chance.

But William had come to ask forgiveness for his brother's indiscretion, and he turned the other cheek to my father's hostility several times over. My dad left in handcuffs, William Hildegard left on a stretcher, bloodied, but the service went on. Joanne's parents had flown in from Connecticut and they weren't about to let anything interrupt the memory of their beloved daughter.

With Dad on his way to jail and no other blood relatives present, no one came looking for Eddie and I. The two sides of the family had never been on good terms, and in hushed whispers they reassured each other that Joanne must have been given good reason to cheat on such a stupid, cheap, fearful man.

The service was short but we stayed hidden under the altar until long after it was over and the pallbearers had taken the casket to the hearse. When my stomach started rumbling I pulled the plate of crackers down into my lap.

"You're not supposed to touch those."

"They're crackers. I'm hungry." I munched a few more down. "You can have some."

"Miss Redford said that they're special and that it makes God sad if we just eat 'em willy nilly."

"That's just something grownups say when they don't want you to do something."

It wasn't long before his stomach began to growl and then we polished them off, but there was no grape juice in sight. Parched and tired, it became clear there was nothing left to do but walk home. I wrestled free of my little suit jacket and ripped off the clip-on tie, throwing them both into the church's dumpster. We took the scenic route through unfenced backyards and alleys, dashing for cover any time we'd set off a motion-sensored flood-light. We passed behind the hardware store where we used to steal leftover scraps of wood to add to our fort.

I was still too stubborn to speak up and comfort him right away. Eddie had disowned me at school because of the seizures. I didn't hate him for that. In fact, looking back I almost understood his need for distance. I guess I wanted him to feel alone for a while.

As we crossed a dimly lit parking lot next to a boarded-up convenience store, he asked me if I thought Mom was going to Hell.

"Why would you think that?"

"Miss Redford says people who sin go to Hell. Didn't Mom sin?"

"I don't know, but if she did, well, she's already burned for it."

He punched me in the arm for that, though I hadn't meant it as a put-down. I was having trouble with the same thoughts myself.

"God's supposed to be nice, right?"

"I guess."

"So, he'll know she was a good mom."

"What if he doesn't? Or what if it doesn't matter?"

"Then God isn't a nice guy."

"But God is love."

"So there's nothing to worry about."

"Okay."

We passed behind the convenience store and cut through a neighbor's backyard and along the side of their house to our street. When we were only a few houses away I realized neither of us had a key. We circled the house twice but had no luck finding a way inside without breaking a window, which we'd then have to pay for with a good lashing. We spent the night in our unfinished fort.

I plucked at the string hanging from the light we'd duct-taped to a ceiling crossmember, but it wouldn't switch on. Dad must've needed the extension cord again. We usually tried to run it along the fence, under the bushes so he couldn't find it very easily. He hated us using electricity for nonessentials, as he called them. I don't remember if there was a moon that night, or clouds, stars, wind, cold, anything outside my direct contact with the old chair—a sidewalk find that still had a FREE sign duct-taped to the arm—and of course, Eddie.

He rested his head on my lap and before long he was shuddering, holding back the sobs until it was more than he could bear. We both cried that night, but the moment only lasted until we fell asleep.

* * *

Somewhere much closer to now, I see Mona for an instant and she can't be mourning. She's wearing a sleeveless dress with delicate flowers along the hem, then a pattern of faint flowers all over. She's holding my hand and then a nurse enters the room with Eddie. Mona smiles reassuringly.

And in a flash we're in our little library room and her face is all contorted with fear and confusion and things are already turning white. Books flying all around. I reach for her arm, my insides screaming, "Get out get out get out," but something breaks the silence of my dream, pulls me back to reality.

Reaching, feeling, probing; fingers racing along waves of cloth and skin, across warm and cold, sensing tubes and cords and bed rails so at least I'm not dead. The heart monitor chirps out my own personal rhythm.

Breathe.

A dull soreness fills my bones, like my skeleton had been removed while I was unconscious, dropped from a building, and then shoved back inside my skin.

How long had I been out? And more importantly, had I dreamed, or were those just the vapors of memories replaying inside a confused, half-conscious mind?

A hand on my hand, then a voice, brings me the rest of the

way back to now. My eyes trace the edges of blurry lights around the room.

"Glad to have you back with us, Mr. Downs. Looks like you had a seizure of some sort. Can you hear me?"

I nod despite the stiffness in my neck, unable to speak as yet. She takes my blood pressure, listens to my breathing and then begins with the usual questions.

Yes, I can feel that.

No, I'm not taking any medications.

No, I don't have any allergies.

Yes, this has happened before.

No, it's definitely not hereditary.

Yes, I can feel that, too.

"Well, you're looking very good. Aside from a couple bruises on your back, I think you'll be on your feet in no time. Your brother came by with a change of clothes. He couldn't stay, but there's a very attractive girl in the waiting room. If you want, I can send her in."

I could literally drive straight out to the middle of Montana and never see another human face again. For the moment, dying alone seems better than trying to outlive such an embarrassment with the one person I'd hoped would never see that side of me.

18:

"This is terrible!" I nearly spit the coffee back into the cup.

"Don't complain. I had to sneak it in as it is. That nurse is a caffeine Nazi."

Mona smiles and sits down next to the bed.

"We could leave, you know. Get some real coffee."

"I think you should listen to the doctors. Give them a little more time to make sure everything is cool. They still don't know what happened."

I know what happened. It's nothing new and it's no big deal, but I can't exactly say so out loud.

All the machines and cords keeping track of my vital signs, I try to follow each one until my eyes blur and Mona shifts on the squeaky hospital chair. I break the silence this time.

"It's a little awkward, all this."

"Just because you're in the hospital at the moment doesn't mean we have to stop our date." She slides my smuggled coffee over and begins to set up a chessboard on my tray. "I found this in the game room."

"Nice. Challenge the invalid to a strategy game."

"Don't think you can get out of this on sympathy. I'll tell the nurse you forced me to get coffee. Against my will. Then she'll take it away and I'll still beat you."

I sip the coffee with reservation.

"You still want to hang around a guy like me?"

"What do you mean, a guy like you?"

I was thinking mainly of the change of clothes on the other guest chair, but I can't breach the subject directly. She reads me well enough.

"Well I'm sure I could tell you some whoppers."

"Indulge me." I try to mimic her curiosity from earlier.

"First, we play chess." She mimics back. "I have to decide if you're someone I can share *my* secrets with."

"Well played."

"Now then, would you like to be black or white?"

"...black?"

"You don't know?"

"Not really. I don't play very well. Why don't you choose?"

"Well, white has the advantage since it always goes first, so why don't you be white?"

It's great to do something other than play twenty questions about my passing out. And to my relief she's not overtly trying to make me feel better. It's like it doesn't even matter.

As we make our first couple moves I ask her something that has bugged me for years, though I have to pretend like it's a newfound curiosity.

"So, you like chess, or...?"

"Yeah, I have about a dozen chess boards."

"Really?" I pause to give the effect of contemplation.

She moves her bishop so it's diagonal from one of my pawns.

"I'm fairly competitive. I try not to be, but sometimes it comes out anyway. I started playing chess to channel that competitiveness into something that would challenge me intellectually instead of socially."

"Oka-ay."

"All the girls my age wanted to play house or dolls. I wanted to take things apart or hike into the woods with the boys, see who could climb a tree the fastest. My mother made every effort to make me more girly, and chess became the only outlet for my competitive nature for a few years.

"But now, I think you can tell a lot about someone by how they play chess. That's why we're playing, if you haven't caught on."

I hadn't.

"So how am I doing?" I move my pawn out of danger and she immediately slides her bishop across the board.

"Checkmate. Only seven moves into the game. That's not so good."

"What does that say about me?"

She began to set the pieces back up.

"That you've had a rough day and you deserve another chance. Relax. This is not a pass/fail kind of test."

She's slowly dismantling my poker face, reading me when I still want to hide things. Before I make my first move this time around she stops me.

"Okay, the idea with chess is this – it's not enough to know what you're going to do. You have to be able to see what your opponent is planning several moves ahead. When I put my bishop there," she points to her second-to-last move, "I hoped you would think that your best possible move was to get your pawn out of harm's way. You did, but by doing so, it made your king vulnerable. It's kind of like misdirection. I want you to worry about some of your pieces but not see the path you're clearing for my attack."

"I'm supposed to second guess what you do."

"Exactly. But a good chess player is also trying to figure out their opponent's strategy. It's not enough to counter only the moves you can see. You need to think five moves ahead."

"My next five moves or yours?"

"Both." She laughs. "You can't just respond to what you observe or you'll be chasing me the whole game and never have a chance. Run away, run away, I'll attack. You'll lose every time."

My stomach sinks.

"So what do I do?"

"That, I can't tell you. It's your move."

"Yeah, I guess you're right."

I'm about to give it another chance when the nurse comes into the room, clearing her throat. Mona deftly hides my caffeinated contraband.

"Mr. Downs, I need to speak with you about, um...well...your insurance."

"What about it?"

"Your policy is...um, it's expired. I'm sorry, but I need to know..."

"Don't worry about it. Will you take a check card?"

"I'm sorry, I don't think you understand. It's a very large bill."

"Try me."

"Well, um, I don't know off the top of my head." The nurse leaves the room, flustered.

"So I'm white this time, right?"

"What kind of drugs have they got you on? You were white last time, too." She giggles. "So you have the advantage, though it hasn't done you any good just yet."

Story of my fucking life.

* * *

I wake up Sunday morning to the sound of my own alarm clock, in my own bed, and I'm feeling good. Not so much physically, but in other ways. Sure, Mona still creamed me in chess. And yeah, my arm still hurts from the IV, and my back is still stiff from the fall.

I feel good because Mona seems to like me in spite of the snags we've run into along the way. We had a real date and I didn't ruin things. If I could end up passing out and in the hospital without her totally losing interest, I'm doing pretty good.

But there was no dream again. I had dreamed something in the hospital while I was out, but I can't be sure if that was anything more than a memory, or maybe a real dream like everyone else has. I muse over the notion of having normal dreams until my snooze timer runs out again.

Autopilot tries to kick in, but halfway through my routine I'm standing in front of an empty space on my countertop for a solid minute unable to process the absence of a coffee maker. Eddie.

Right. I finally get past that detail and do the whole clothes, phone, wallet, keys thing and begin walking to work. I'm glad the weather has warmed back up, but I'm jolted out of my five AM daze by a sign that reads:

Future site of The Spy House
Grand Opening: Tuesday, 7pm!
02 more days!

David must have known all along. We're all unemployed now but he was already selling the place. There's no way they're having a grand opening so soon unless they'd had all their plans ready to go months ago.

Back at my apartment I stare at the empty spot on my counter again, and the good feeling I had when I woke up is fading. The closest source of caffeine won't be open for another hour and I don't feel like falling back to sleep.

My cell phone is blinking: new voicemails. Heath's number comes up on the missed call log, then Shelley's, then David's, and two more from Shelley.

It's too early to think, too early to listen to messages without caffeine in me to clarify the details from the static. Sitting on the couch I flip on the TV and try to stay awake but it doesn't help. I'm feeling shaky within a half hour. Desperate, I forage through the kitchen for a clean spoon and pull a bag of coffee grounds out of the freezer. It's come to this.

On the back porch, spitting excess juice like chewing tobacco, waiting for sunrise, my lips feel funny and in a few minutes even my scalp begins to tingle. I probably have enough grounds for three full mugs stuffed into my face. Part of me is repulsed, but another part of me wonders why I've never tried this before. My cell rings.

"Hey, Ezekiel. Jim-Bo. What happened to Gallagher's?"

"You haven't heard?"

"I was home."

"Right. I'll be over in a minute." At five-thirty in the morning, company is company. Jim's sitting on one of only three chairs left when I get there.

"What did I tell you? People will steal anything that isn't locked up. This place got shut down Friday, middle of the day. No one thought to worry about the furniture, now it's almost gone."

I spit out a black-brown glob. "Coffee maker's busted." I smile, my teeth rough with dregs.

"What happened?"

I hock the last of the grounds into the bushes.

"My brother is an idiot, so—"

"No, I mean here."

"Oh...money problems. I really don't know. But it's not so bad. I bet there are plenty of places within walking distance that are still hiring for the semester."

"What are you going to do?"

"Not to sound cliché, but I'm taking it one day at a time right now."

And that's when I remember the hospital bill has just set me back nearly ten grand. Just like last summer. What's the point of knowing the future when history repeats itself?

* * *

"Hey, man, where can I find an iced coffee?" Eddie wakes me up.

"I don't know, man. What time is it?"

"Nine-ish. Look, man, with your place closed, and I am sorry about that, but I really need some coffee."

I don't even remember going home or falling asleep. Now I find myself in a lump of bed sheets on the couch. "There's the Freight House Dunn Bros on 3rd and Washington. They should have it."

"Thanks, man."

"I thought you hated that stuff." I nod toward the trashcan, brimming with plastic cups.

"I don't exactly love smoking either. But nicotine calms me down and caffeine keeps me going. Later." He vanishes out the door.

I tongue around inside my mouth, looking for a hint of coffee grounds. Nothing. I'm feeling off and the room is not exactly still. My vision gets a little shaky as Eddie storms back down the stairs.

"Forgot my frequent-buyer's card." He holds it up and it's nearly full of little coffee-bean-shaped holes. "You okay?"

"Yeah, just a little out of it."

"I'll say. You slept all day yesterday and now you look like shit."

"Wait, what day is it?"

"It's Monday, man. Like I said, you were out cold."

"Fuck me sideways."

"Uh... I don't know what that means, but..."

"Look, I need some caffeine, too. Why don't I give you a ride."

"Cool."

"Do you need a ride to work, too? I notice you're late."

"No man, it's a bank holiday."

"Shit! That's right." Labor Day. The last day of the last week of live racing at Canterbury. My last guaranteed payday for, well shit, maybe forever if I'm not careful.

"What's right?"

"Nothing. Never mind. Let's hit it."

* * *

I'm holding on to the counter, trying to keep the words on the menu from shaking when a familiar voice says, "So you don't answer your phone anymore."

"Shelley?"

"Yeah. They were looking for help. I got Jim an interview tomorrow. They don't need a roaster but you could probably get some hours behind the counter."

"That's great. Thanks." I scramble. "So, you're not upset about..."

"No." She looks away. "It wasn't your fault."

"You haven't heard from Allison, have you?"

"No, thank God. I'm sure she got the news from David, though."

"Hey there, Shelley." Eddie pops out from behind me.

Shelley's eyes ice over.

"Hello."

Eddie shrinks back.

"So, what'll it be?"

"Two iced coffees, easy on the ice."

"For you? Or has Lefty converted?"

Eddie peeks out from behind me, holding up his hole-punched frequent-buyer's card.

"I'm officially hooked."

"Well, I suppose everyone has to have a good side."

Eddie and I find a table upstairs, and of course the first thing out of his mouth is, "Dude, she said I have a good side. Do you think she'd ever go out with me?"

"Considering recent events?"

"Right." He takes a long sip. "So what are you up to today?"

"Nothing, I guess."

"Liar." He smiles like he knows something.

"What?"

"What are the odds you'll be heading out to Canterbury this afternoon?"

I shrug like I haven't thought about it.

"Come on, man. I'm not stupid."

"Okay, I'll be there, but you're not coming so forget about it."

"I don't want to go. I just want you to be straight with me. I'm sorry about your job, really. But other than that I thought we were getting along lately."

"We weren't. I was tolerating you until you got a new place. How's that coming along, anyway?"

"I'm still nearly broke, man. It's going to be a couple weeks before I even get my cell phone paid up."

"Well, you're on your own there."

"I wasn't going to ask, you jackass."

"Oh yeah, right, you're turning over a new leaf. Isn't that what you said last summer? And here we are again."

"God, I'd hate to think my own brother might be able to help out. I'm trying, okay."

"Half-brother."

"Screw you." He shoves away from the table. And all I can think is, *I may not make it, so you're going to have to learn to swim on your own.*

"Hey, man. I am not your savior. I'm just as fucked as you."

"Please," he says, his voice thick with sarcasm, "don't take pity on me."

And he's already walking away, but I go on. "I can't save you, Eddie. I can't even save myself."

19:

It starts off like a halfway decent Labor Day. I get coffee with my brother and tell him to take care of his own problems. He consents, though not without some attitude. Then I 'happen' to come across Mona reading in the park, only this time she's sitting on the bench, which has never happened before. In my dreams, I mean.

I invite her out on a Labor Day date, but she says there's class today, only the big universities have the day off. I tell her it's a special event because this is the last day we could do what I have in mind until next year, and at that she's convinced it must be better than sitting through Statistics and Psychology.

I keep her in suspense the entire drive, her face aglow with anticipation until we pull into the lot. When I aim for the handicapped spot she seems to be getting tense.

"This is a joke, right?"

I pull out the blue placard and hang it in the rear-view mirror, saying, "No joke, I'm allowed to park here." Little white lies. I instantly feel bad. "Okay, it's my dad's blue window thingy."

"No, not that. I mean, this is a casino, right?" She changes from reticent to downright annoyed. "This is your idea of a date?"

"Well, no. We're here for the horses."

I expect her to light up at that, figuring, girls like horses. Nothing changes.

"Please tell me this is not what it looks like."

I even take a moment to explain my whole gambling vs. investment philosophy. I tell her that it was horse racing that took care of my hospital bill the other day, and it's helped bail Eddie out a couple times, too.

"Well, let's get in there, then."

Mona gets out and slams the door. I flinch, waiting for

something to fall off the car, but she's already bulldozing her way inside and I'm scrambling to keep up until she stops, scoping out the crowd.

She pulls me right over to the most pathetic-looking old man she can find, hunched over in a powered wheelchair with an oxygen tank on the back. Drooling into a warm beer like he's been there for weeks, half awake. He doesn't notice us.

"It's his money you're taking. From him and his grandkids and his wife, if she's still alive. This is what you do for fun?"

The old man grumbles something and slowly rolls away. I try to pull her aside, saying, "Take it easy. I thought you'd like seeing the horses up close."

She goes on like nothing I've said even registers.

"It doesn't matter if you're really good with your picks. It doesn't matter if you're making money. You have to realize that if people like this old man didn't lose, you wouldn't have any money to make. Your success is at their expense. Look around. You called Eddie a leech the other day—"

"Whoa. Easy. Hold on."

"Hold on? Wake up. The world isn't just your personal playground. Actions have consequences."

"Jesus, what are you, my mom?"

"Don't you mean step-mom?"

"My mom died giving birth to me."

"Well I'm still breathing, so that rules me out, doesn't it?" She draws back the moment her words die in the air between us. "Alright, I shouldn't—"

"Save it."

"Hey, look, I know what that's li—"

"You don't have any fucking idea what it's like. I've been through more shit than you could ever dream about. You, with your scholarship trust fund shit—"

"Go to Hell."

"Yeah, you know, I Googled Hell. Sounds like a real shitty

place, so no thanks. Especially since I'd have to share it with—"

Now I'm an idiot.

There's a long pause. She draws back and her face goes dead blank.

"Wait, what do you mean? How could you know that?"

Fuck. Fuck. Fuck. "Know what?"

"You know. Exactly. What I'm talking about."

"Shit."

"You just...you stay away from me."

She pulls out her cell phone and disappears into the crowd.

* * *

Heath takes a contemplative breath, rubbing his chin even though it's shaved clean today. We're sitting at a bench in Elliot Park, classes are about to let out, and I can't tell if it's hot or I'm just sweating due to nerves.

After a long pause he asks, "How did that make you feel?"

"Look, I don't need you to examine me. I need you to help me figure this out."

"What do you want me to say? She had a good point about the horse racing."

"God, everyone's against me." I throw my hands in the air.

"Relax. I'm on your side. We just need to figure out how to get back on track so you two can have your happily-ever-after."

We both laugh, but it's tentative.

"Okay, tell me that doesn't sound ridiculous. And highly unlikely. Especially now that she knows that I know more about her than I should."

"Right, you did dig yourself into a hole with that."

"I've been digging for years, apparently."

"Well, you are the king of long shots."

"Correction – I used to be the king of long shots. Like I said, I'm all messed up. I'm not dreaming, I'm not feeling anything anymore. I don't even know if I'd have made money today or not. All these things, I haven't seen anything coming."

"Like running into me?"

"Yeah, for starters. Losing my job. Ending up in the hospital. Eddie moving in. Gallagher's shutting down. I didn't have a clue."

"We'll figure something out." He glances at his watch. "Look, I have a barbecue at five, so I need to take off." He walks over to his car and I follow.

"You think I've still got a chance?"

"I don't know, but we can hope." He smiles like a good counselor always does, but when he opens the back door to toss his coat inside, for a split second I see about a dozen notebooks and what looks like a white wig on the floor of the back seat. Then there's a pair of giant, old-person sunglasses, the kind that fit over your regular glasses. I pull my backpack free of my shoulder, weighing it in my hand.

It makes sense. In this moment of real, tangible time, one more thing finally makes sense. It's just too much of a coincidence that he looked me up out of the blue.

My eyes tell his eyes I know, and his eyes tell mine, *Oh shit*. He folds his glasses up and puts them in his shirt pocket. Too bad I left his silver pen on my dresser this morning. He shuts the door and doesn't even try to run while every muscle and sinew in my body prepares for combat.

I take him by the throat and whip him back to the table, my sudden burst of adrenaline-fueled anger overpowering the man. I pin him against the table, my knee on his chest, getting down so close to his face I can feel the fear evaporating out of his sweat glands.

I whisper, "What the Hell is this?"

"A b-book...I wanted to write a b-b-book. Just let me...explain..."

"Indulge me." I loosen my grip on his neck slightly. He does his best to compose himself.

"You saved my life. You're one of a kind. You aren't supposed to even exist, but...you obviously do. I want to tell your story."

"My story?"

"Yeah. I want the world to know about you."

"But it's my life. My story. What's going to keep me from telling it?"

"I wasn't sure if...you know...how it would end. I didn't want to take any chances."

"You want to tell my story because you think...I won't be here to tell it."

I tense and bear down with all my weight and he tries to wrestle free.

"In that case, you'd better leave out the chapter on my kidnapping, huh?"

He tries to say the word, *Help*. His eyes dash every direction, looking for someone to notice.

"Were you going to get some sort of made-for-TV movie deal? Huh?"

"No, not at first...I mean, we hadn't made any plans."

"We?!"

"You don't want to do this."

"I don't know. Maybe you should call your agent, ask him. This could be a really exciting chapter. The main character strangles the writer and writes his own ending."

"You have to die, Zeek... It's what happens to guys like you. There are only a few stories out there, ever. This," gasp, "this is your story. It's a tragedy."

"You may want to edit the following scene, too."

The bell rings and students begin to flood out of the school, but it's just our faces, nose to nose, predator and prey. If this were a movie the camera would zoom out and pan up, allowing only the sound of bone and meat and wood, the reaction on the faces of college kids walking by fill in the blanks.

Heath is smart enough to not report me for assault. He knows that I'd turn him in for kidnapping, saying that he was the same man I'd reported for molesting me all those years ago. I'd tell the cops he must have come back for revenge. The police records are all there, waiting to be resurrected. Heath's not a genius, but he's not that stupid.

I'm home, I don't know how much time has passed. Almost done putting my notebooks in order when I hear Eddie coming down the stairs. They're not all here. There are gaps, huge gaps, gone, who knows where?

The door opens and shuts, Eddie stops in his tracks.

"Holy shit, man. Are you studying already?"

"Just...organizing."

"You look pissed."

"I am pissed."

He picks up a notebook and begins to flip through before I realize. I stand and square off the way I always have when I'm about to take him down.

"Drop it."

He laughs, but it's cut short.

"Is that your blood?"

"Some of it, yeah." I stand, lean close. "Someone wouldn't give back one of my journals earlier today."

Eddie drops the notebook.

"Okay, okay, I got it. But why haven't you, you know...changed clothes? You look like Hell."

"It's my new favorite shirt. You don't like it?"

"You're freaking me—"

"Get what you need and get the Hell out of here."

* * *

I call Mona's room a couple times, but only get a generic voicemail and I don't bother leaving a message. I figure she probably found someone to blab to about what a weirdo I'd turned out to be. Nice guy at first, but he stutters, and then that gambling problem. The AG doesn't smile on those kinds of people. My kind of people.

Maybe it was all misdirection. All this time I've been worried about having coffee in a library with a girl who adores me. Instead, she thinks I'm a leech. Not Eddie. Me. And it doesn't look like we'll be sharing a cup of Joe any time soon. Maybe we were supposed to be breaking up in that café, but it happened at Canterbury instead.

Right now, in this actual moment of real, tangible time, I'm feeling scared and hopeless and lost just like every other man, woman and child on this fucking planet, ducking around every corner, waiting for God to finally drop an anvil on my head and be done with it all.

20:

Here's me this morning, half awake, light swinging above my head, hands cramped from writing all night, filling in the gaps to make up for the missing journals. Here I am today, right now, back in the real world, the unknown, wrists aching from a pair of handcuffs slapped on too tight, sitting in the backseat of a police cruiser. This isn't fate. It's just my luck.

I woke up late. The clock said, *Who cares if it's six in the AM? Go ahead and roll over again, you've got nowhere to be but dead.* Without dreaming my bullshit future for the last few days I've been sleeping pretty well. I just close my eyes and the next thing I know it's tomorrow.

"Hey, buddy, you up?" Eddie peeks in my door saying, "I got this for you." He jiggles a plastic cup that glistens with condensation.

"Really?"

"Yeah, why not? I'm turning over a new leaf, remember?"

I take the iced coffee and decide to go for a walk. They've stripped the Gallagher's logo from the big front window of where I used to work. Now this guy is painting a big red, seventies style graphic of cross hairs right below the 'e' of Spy House. He's outlined a retro-style man with a briefcase sneaking away in the corner. Their grand-opening sign declares 'Tonight, tonight, tonight!' Fucking David. Knew all along.

I follow 11th avenue until I come to 6th street. To my left is the stadium and beyond that, downtown, so I take a right, the on-ramp for I-94.

I stay to the left, the car-pool lane, and I consider my options. I could rot away in my apartment and wait for my money to run out, just like Dad. I could get a job and work the rest of my life, never knowing what's going to happen from moment to moment; a nervous wreck. I could walk straight to Hell,

Michigan and explain to Mr. Whoever that Mona is going to die and I was supposed to be able to stop it but for all the time I've had I haven't come up with a single bright idea. I could say there's a good chance we were supposed to die together like a proper Greek tragedy, but I can't even be sure of that anymore.

"Just tell your daughter, if she's not already dead, that is, to avoid libraries. So she needs to move. Pronto."

All this, of course, would be contingent on fate not catching up with me at some point in the next couple days.

I suppose I could jump off the overpass. I spit over the edge and wind carries the glob twenty or so feet diagonal before it smacks silently into the pavement. No. I don't even have the guts to start smoking, not really, and leaping from a bridge is definitely something I'd have seen coming.

I sit in the car-pool lane and close my eyes, thrilled at the thought of anything catching up with me, here, now, and I'd never know. Will it be a bus? A family sedan?

Commuters are trying to merge onto the highway. Eyes closed. Horns honking. The occasional screech. I never flinch. One car after another goes around me and I feel the whoosh as it passes and smell the exhaust. They don't have the guts to hit me, and I don't have the guts to jump.

Finally some concerned citizen calls the cops and they sit me down on the curb, asking if I'm high or drunk, and I suppose after a couple days without so much as a shower, sucking on coffee grounds to stay awake, I'm looking pretty damn strung out.

"What day is it, anyway?"

"You don't know what day it is, Mr.—" he opens my wallet, "—Mr. Downs? Is that your real name?"

"Ezz-z-z-z-z-ekiel. I'm Ezekiel D-downs."

"Okay, Mr. Downs. Today is Tuesday. Do you know where you are?"

"I was heading for I-94, b-but I changed my mind."

"What were you going to do on the 94?"

"Just walk."

"Anywhere in particular?"

"Hell, maybe. I really had no plan, you know?"

Staring blankly at me, he doesn't seem to know.

"Oka-ay. Well, we can't have you walking on the highway, sir. Mind explaining what you're doing with that spoon?"

It's sticking out of my pocket.

"Uh..."

They take it, each smelling it carefully, like it's some sort of evidence.

"Smells like...coffee."

"Tanzania Peaberry. Full City roast." I smile.

"So, what do you think?" The first cop doesn't seem sure what to make of me, a disheveled guy with a stutter just sitting in the middle of the road.

"Let's take him downtown. I mean, his record's clean, maybe he's..." the second cop crosses his eyes, "...you know."

"You come with us, Mr. Downs. We'll get you sorted out."

* * *

They let me go after a couple hours of psycho-babble questions from a guy who seemed to care more about his tie being straight than anything I was saying. He kept checking his watch, showing off his cufflinks, crossing and re-crossing his legs so I could marvel at his expensive shoes and how his socks accented the pattern on his tie. He's probably pissed he's gotten such a shitty job after going through so many years of college. Really nice pen, too. Reminded me of Heath's.

Having broken no laws and posing no apparent threat to others or myself, they drop me off on my corner around ten in the morning. I click on the TV.

News. News. Commercial. News. Then some auto auction

with all these classic cars lined up, boasting low original miles or hundred-thousand-dollar restorations. It all feels so hollow. What's the point of owning a Ferrari if you never drive it? Car after car, people bid in increments larger than everything I earned last year. These folks are spending more than most people will earn in their entire life to buy a car they'll park in a garage and bring out one or two sunny days a year.

I'm about to click away when an entire row of Cobras catches my eye. Dark blue, some with racing stripes, some without, the painted grey wheels and tiny doors, wooden steering wheels: ten of them altogether, to be auctioned off throughout the event.

And then it hits me. That's David standing by one of the Cobras. Jesus, he must be desperate.

The man on the screen is saying something and even though the TV is muted his words are obvious, he's saying, "original," then there's a shot of a wheel or a dashboard, then smashcut back to the same guy, now he's saying "replica," and there's a shot of an engine bay, he's saying, "tell tale signs," and "one of the best replicas we've ever seen," then there's a shot of him talking to David and some man with a grey blazer holding a stack of paperwork. I click up the volume in time to catch the voice-over saying, "—is that these are getting more and more difficult to catch. Many owners have bought these cars completely unaware—" and I have to click away because the look on David's face is too much to bear and I can't spend another second worried about his shit.

I click away and it only gets worse. Car crashes, weight loss tips, manufacturer's recalls, hurricane on the East Coast, and won't you please donate to the emaciated children's fund of butt-fucking Egypt?

Just like all those poor starving kids with flies crawling around their sticky eyes and swollen bellies, I know what it's like to think, *If only I could reach my next birthday.*

The higher the channel, the higher the stakes. There's a special on the Crusades, then World War II, something about the Plague. Even the Weather Channel is in on the tragedy angle with a series on the greatest natural disasters so far, followed immediately by a series on disasters that hadn't even happened yet, but could happen tomorrow. Everyone thrives on conflict. We eat it up as if we've got nothing better to do than immerse ourselves in the misery of others. Reality shows, real police chases that end horribly, shocking home videos where a kid falls from a skateboard and breaks his arm or an old lady crosses the road and gets creamed by a bus.

I come back around to the auto auction and here's another story about a guy in Germany who made fake Porsches, classics, and all the people he's ripped off, many of them finding out for the first time on live television, right now for your viewing pleasure.

Acts of God, Darwin awards, total devastation in High Definition and I've seen it all. I stopped visiting crash sites before they happened years ago. I stopped watching houses burn down or electrical workers touch the wrong wire. I got bored.

I zombie into the kitchenette and there's still a relatively clean spot where my coffee maker should be. The TV cackles away in the background about the extended forecast, or something. There should be a coffee shop open somewhere. Life is short, may as well be awake for the finale.

* * *

Now here's Eddie sitting down with Shelley in my living room showing his concern, saying something about classic depression symptoms. Between the two of them, they decide they have some really good ideas, but I'm just sucking on coffee grounds, pulling the switch on and off above me and channel surfing, so Eddie regroups, tries another angle.

"Any plans for today?"

He's got that optimism in his voice again. He's only asking me this as a segue to something he wants me to know.

"Nope. And what about you?"

"Not much. Heading over to The Spy House at seven, for the grand opening."

"I think it's stupid to have a grand opening at night."

"I don't know. It's supposed to go with their whole cloak-and-dagger theme. It goes until 2 AM."

I'd been telling David to stay open later, that college students would spend tons if they knew they could study till those prime creative hours after ten. Idiot.

"Oh, and tomorrow I have an apartment to look at."

"Really?"

"Found a place near work, a studio. It's in the Warehouse District, so it's not super tiny, but the rent's still cheap. And I won't have to take the bus anymore 'cause it's so close."

"Good. Proud of you."

We watch the Weather Channel for a while, and it seems like we're on the same side again.

"Hey, whatever happened with you and that girl you were hanging around?"

I'm avoiding her because I can no longer see the future and I don't want to die. But I don't say that, of course.

"I saw you guys together once or twice. I know you were crushing on her, so don't try to get out of it. Shelley filled me in here and there, too. What's shaking?"

"Nothing. She pretty much hates me."

"Why?"

"She has this moral dilemma about horse racing."

"Animal lover?"

"No. She made a scene about me stealing money from helpless old guys and, well..."

"Guys like me."

"If you mean guys with shitty luck, then yeah. Anyway, things really went south out at Canterbury the other day."

"Well? I mean, is that it?"

"I don't know. Maybe. Yes. No. Who knows? What do you care?"

He waits for a moment, but something in his tone is off. He's too eager, leaning forward on the couch, saying, "You should call her. Tell her you're sorry for being a jerk and try to start things over." He smiles with a bit too much confidence.

"What aren't you telling me?"

He reaches into his jacket, saying, "Nothing. You want a smoke?"

"What aren't you telling me?"

"That Mona's sitting in the park right now, and Shelley ran into her last night, and, well, you should probably go to patch things up. Do I have to spell it out?"

Shelley simply nods.

* * *

Picture me walking faster than usual, all geared up and ready to win Mona back. The blind optimism on my face must be hilarious. I wait around the corner from the park, behind the T.J. Jones Memorial Library, watching her read and wondering what I might say that won't make her think I'm out of my mind.

I make my approach.

The afternoon breeze moves through her hair as the sun's dying rays fill it with sparks of auburn and red I hadn't noticed before.

"About time for a refill?"

"Actually, I just got this." She lies, which surprises me. Her face seems flushed, maybe a little embarrassed about our last exchange.

I wait, hoping she might make the next move, but nothing happens. Before the silence becomes unbearable I go for it.

"I'm really sorry about yesterday."

"You kind of flipped out."

"Right. Look, I d-didn't know how you felt about..."

She sighs heavily, closing her book.

"Don't be sorry. I shouldn't have snapped like that. I don't even know what the big deal was. I've grown up being told certain things were, well..."

"Evil?"

"Yeah. Smoking, drinking, gambling." She sighs. "Dancing."

I nod along with her list of evils, adding, "The Smurfs."

"You're kidding."

"Nope, I was never allowed to watch the Smurfs because I had a Sunday-school teacher who was convinced they were evil."

She laughs and a mountain of tension lifts. She hasn't brought up the whole knowledge thing but I'm tense, waiting for it to come back to her.

"Look, Mona, there is so much I want you to know about me."

"Okay, just. No. Haven't you ever seen a chick flick?"

"What?"

"You're supposed to say, 'There's so much I want to know about you.' Meaning me, of course." She smiles.

"That too."

"Though it appears you've done you're homework already. Who was it, anyway?"

"Who was what?"

"You know. Who did you get to?"

"I..."

"Was it Charity? She talks too much, I could tell the moment she sat down she was a gossip."

"Well..."

"Anyway, I just love the fact that I can tell these sheltered little church girls I grew up in Hell, no really, Hell, it's a real place, Hell, Michigan. I guess I didn't keep it a secret."

I nod, which I suppose is half a lie, but I need this.

"So are we all right?"

"Give me some time."

"Actually, that's one of the things we need to talk about. We're running out of time. I mean, I know I am, and you probably are too, but..."

Her face twists. "You say the weirdest things."

"Look, I know it sounds completely fucked up, but do you think we could talk somewhere?"

"We're talking here, aren't we?"

"Right."

I can tell Shelley has convinced her to give me another chance, but her guard is ready to go back up any moment. It's now or never, because more than anything, I need freedom from all the things I know. And I need at least one person I can be honest with in this fucked-up world.

I look deep into her eyes and the levee breaks.

"I know you, Mona. I know things about you I shouldn't know. It wasn't your roommate, or anyone on your floor. And it's nothing like what you're thinking right now, just listen."

"What are you talking about?"

"Listen, this is important. Things weren't supposed to happen this way. I was supposed to show you where Financial Aid was, but Eddie needed help that afternoon. That threw everything off. You got hung up with that Josh kid, and I'm sorry about that, believe me. Then I was supposed to t-take a walk with you that night, but you didn't show up. Your plane was delayed, and I can't even begin to figure out how that changed. I know we did, we took a walk together, but it was a d-day late."

She starts to get up.

"Look, I think it'd be better if we..."

I pull her into my arms and go on.

"You have to listen. We were supposed to play chess, but not in the hospital, and then you would tell me about this one set that your brother brought back for you from Angola. And the

Celtic one your father gave you."

"What are you trying to—Who are you?"

"Aren't those things true?"

She nods.

"You told me those things, Mona. And about how you hate eating pizza crust and how...you flew to Peru one time just for the day and then came back, because you had an airline voucher that was about to expire."

"I haven't told—"

"Then you're supposed to ask me why I stutter sometimes, and I would tell you that it's because I had a really rough year in third grade. I'm supposed to tell you that my stepmother died that fall, and then on the last day of school I killed my teacher. I killed her...that was the day my stuttering began. She died right in front of me. It was just a stray bullet but I made her...

"God, Mona, my whole world crashed in, she collapsed in front of me...the sound of the gun was so loud and everyone was screaming and I killed her... We're supposed to have this whole conversation and then we're in this room, some library, with coffee, and now you live in a library...

"I've been dreaming about you since I was nine years old because you're always there when I die and I was hoping all my life that you'd be able to save me. And now I realize that it was me who needed saving."

I collapse into hopeless sobs and I'm alone. I never even feel her slip away from my arms. Her book lies next to me, her coffee is all over the ground and she's nowhere in sight. Nothing happens.

I jump at every sound, every time the wind changes or a crow skulks by, every hand-of-death shadow that the setting sun casts long and dark over across the park lawn.

* * *

"Well, that blew up in my face." I take a cigarette from Eddie, hands shaking.

"What happened?"

"I may as well get honest with you, too."

"Jesus, Zeek. You make it sound like the world is coming to an end."

"For me it is."

"What are you—?"

"First, let me tell you about my horse-betting system."

"Really?"

"Yeah. The whole truth."

I don't even bother looking at his face. I don't know what parts he believes or not. It didn't feel nearly as cathartic, spilling my guts to Eddie when the only person I wanted to be honest with had run off the moment I opened up to her. I talk and talk, chain-smoking three cigarettes until I throw up in the bushes.

"But now I know, I'm supposed to save her," I wipe my mouth with my sleeve, "and I don't know how. Eddie, I don't know how. All my life...it's been meaningless."

"Zeek, I hate to interrupt you, but did you mean what you said about your teacher?"

"Yeah, why?"

"You're not going to believe this."

He holds out Mona's copy of Inferno, the one she left on the ground. I'd picked it up. It smelled like her. Eddie holds it out and flips the cover open to a stamp, the sort of thing a real book collector would have in each of their books. And there it is. My glass ceiling breaks and the thought nearly crushes my mind.

21:

Every time the sickness pushes up my throat I scorch it back with another cigarette. Suddenly I like the feeling of burning from the inside. I control the burn and that power is exhilarating, like sucking fumes from the barrel of a gun. I've spent my life flirting with death but I've always been too scared to take the reins until right this moment.

We kill the last of his Marlboro's in a half hour, and all Eddie can think to say is, "Man, this is heavy."

"I know. And she already thinks I'm a lunatic. It's what I get for being honest."

I grab an empty bottle and chuck it against the driveway.

"I'm telling you, you should just walk right in there and find her, man."

"She lives in the most secure building on campus. It's not going to happen."

Eddie almost comes out of his skin, jumping off the porch. The sun just low enough now, cue the motion-sensored floodlight, spotlighting Eddie for his big moment of inspiration.

"What if it's not the dorm? What if it's not the library?"

"What are you talking about?"

"What if you just assumed..." He trails off.

"She lives on the third floor of the library. That's the girls honor dorm. In a library. And that's my dream. In a library."

He's hopping around, totally unfazed.

"Yeah, but right now she's probably at The Spy House."

"How do you know that?"

"Because I ran into her earlier and asked her what she was up to tonight. She said her roommate was signed up for the open mic and all their friends were going to show support."

"So?"

"Then I explained that I wasn't hitting on her, and that's when

Shelley stepped in and told her how sorry you were about whatever had happened and that you talk about her all the time and you—"

"Get to the point."

"Have you even seen the new place?"

"Of course not."

"I mean, you haven't looked in the windows or anything?"

"Jesus fucking Christ!"

He grabs my arm with his one good hand, practically shouting, "You have to see this. It changes everything."

Fast forward past me grabbing my backpack, with all the notebooks I could find, scrambling to stash them somewhere Heath will never think to look, just in case Eddie is right. Just in case things go south. Skim over the two blocks it takes to get to The Spy House as Eddie explains that while I was busy convincing Mona I was some creepy stalker, he was dividing his time between spying on the two of us and peeking inside the windows of the newly remodeled coffee shop. We walk right to where the door should be but there's no handle.

"It's over here."

Eddie walks to the new entrance on the far left of the shop. The new door has a sign on it that reads: PASSWORD: JAVA. I roll my eyes.

Inside, the place is packed and it takes me a second to realize that everything is backwards. The walls have gone from blues and greens to this black and maroon color scheme. The counter is still the same, but the menus are rearranged and the drinks all have these clichéd names. The best was the decaf menu, labeled: The Big Sleep. I don't recognize anyone behind the counter, but they all sport nametags that start with, 'Codename:' and their names are in all caps. Looks like JOSHUA has struck again.

The biggest difference is that the part of the room where the front door used to be is now partitioned off with walls that don't quite reach the ceiling and a curtain across the entrance. There's a sign that says: Strategic Planning Headquarters.

The old community room is now simply labeled, Music Room, on a ten-by-twelve piece of white paper. I guess they haven't come up with a spy-themed name for that one yet.

And then there's JOSHUA clutching his guitar, and I recognize about a half dozen faces, mostly Asbury students. Mr. Blue Glasses, Bethany, Shelley, even a couple kids from the Worship Live! And right next to the door are the two girls whose dad had clipped the parked car with his trailer that Sunday afternoon. Shit, maybe this is their fault.

"Hey, that's the guy who set this whole thing up tonight." Eddie is pointing at JOSHUA. "Lucky for you, Mona's roommate wants to impress him with her singing, or else Mona probably wouldn't be here."

"Fantastic. Where's Mona?"

"Right this way." Eddie points toward the Strategic Planning Room, but JOSHUA intercepts me en-route.

"Hey, Zeek, you got a minute?"

"Actually, I might not."

He leans in close enough for me to feel his breath, saying, "It's been killing me, man. Do people really say that stuff about me?"

"I don't know. Who do you mean by people?"

"People. You know. People."

"Some. I guess. Look-"

"Oh, man." He looks like he's about to cry, so I grab him by the arm and pull him over to a wall to get out of the crowd.

"Look, screw everyone, Josh. Forget about them. You think I give a d-damn about what people think about me?"

His eyes go distant. "Is that what you think of me?"

"Why do you care what I think? Who the fuck am I?"

"Everyone is talking about you, the new guy, and that girl you're always with. People seem to care what you say. I guess I wish that..."

"Wait, what? Me?"

"It's a small school, stuff gets around. If there's one thing Bible college is good for, it's rumors. You're one of the most eligible freshmen."

I take a step back.

"...and you didn't even know it, did you?"

"Wow. I can't say I saw that coming."

"So you never answered me. What do you think?"

It looks like this is going to happen so I let loose.

"I think you're an idiot."

He stares like a stunned animal, waiting for the deathblow.

"Josh, you play guitar better than most of the people I've ever tried to jam with. 'Giant Steps?' Are you fucking kidding me?

"Look, I know music theory, but that's it. Now you want me to believe that you've gotten that good for no reason, that it's something you do in your spare time? Something you don't care about?"

"Well..."

"No way, man. No excuses. Why the Hell are you studying to be a pastor? Do you even care about that half as much as you care about music?"

He glances down at his guitar case, that bumper sticker about being a light to the world.

"I'd be fourth generation, man. You don't understand what that means. It's what we do in my family."

I nod to the bumper sticker myself.

"Your family, they all want you to be a light? How does doing something you love interfere with that? Why not try to be your own light for a while?"

Three people push past us into the Music Room.

"I don't know."

"Think of what that's going to mean to your kid, when he's pressured into being the fifth generation, only he's an artist or a history buff or, shit, I don't know, a coffee roaster."

"It's not that easy. I mean, I have one year left. I can't up and change my major now. I'm stuck."

"Josh, man, there's probably twenty-five, thirty-thousand dollars' worth of music equipment in that room, in the hands of idiots. Half of them are probably studying music and will never know music the way you do already. Music is a language to guys like us. A language I interpret but you seem to speak fluently."

"But I can't quit."

"Fuck you then. Finish your preaching degree. I'm sure it will look great on your wall."

My heart is racing, but somehow I give a shit about this kid at the moment. Maybe I can't fix everything, but I'm living right now, winging it. Anything can happen, and I feel like I need the momentum if I'm going to face Mona again.

"Ezekiel, you know it's funny. I honestly expected to come over here and you'd tell me off. Then I'd say sorry you feel that way and I'd be totally justified thinking you were a jerk."

"I was a jerk. I was having a shitty night..."

He looks like he wants a man-hug, so I step aside, saying, "You don't need a degree to prove what you can already do. Now, I hate to cut this short, but I have a very pressing matter at hand."

"It's cool. See you around."

"I hope so."

I immediately grab Eddie by the shoulders.

"Seriously. Where is she?"

He leads me to the Strategic Planning Room and as we push the veil aside, I realize that these aren't new walls. They're bookshelves.

Mona looks up from her coffee with tears tracing black lines down her cheeks. She's sitting along the back wall of the room, streetlights throw the crosshairs of The Spy House logo across the wall, across her, across hundreds of books and thousands of dreams. Cue the mood-setting thunder rumbling in the background.

I slide her copy of Inferno across the table, opening the cover.

"You know Fiore means flower?"

She looks away. "How long have you known? About my mother?"

"About a half hour. I am so sorry."

The smallest chuckle squeaks out between sobs. I thought it was a sarcastic laugh, I thought she was about to tell me off, but slowly she begins to smile.

"I've wondered all these years how my life would be different if my mom were alive. You have no idea what it was like."

"I'll listen, if..."

"She was a horrible woman."

I choose my words carefully.

"You know, I spent most of that school year in the utility closet...b-because she didn't want to d-deal with me."

"You must have been the kid who shit himself. Just like in Elliot Park the other day."

My face feels hot, but we've got no time for pride.

"Guilty."

"Yeah, well, at my house, those closets had doors." Her eyes glaze over. "And locks. Once, she forgot about me until the next morning. Once..." She stares off again. "A few times."

As she tells me about a manipulative, controlling mother who I knew as Mrs. Fury, it's like years of pain wash over her face, but once it's all out there in the open she sighs like it's all been somehow purged.

"She hated that about me. The competitive streak, how I always played with boys. She wanted me to sing and play dolls and take ballet. Not long after she died, my father bought me my first chess set. He taught me how to be a lady, yet still be me. I can't imagine how they even got together in the first place."

"I still feel like shit about all this. I mean..."

"No. Don't." She reaches toward my hand but stops herself. "If anything, I felt guilty when she died. I was almost relieved. I cried for her, you know, I grieved. She was my mom. But I also felt...free."

Mona takes my hand. "I forgive you."

Cue the fade to white.

What seems like a set of high beams floods the room and tells me that this Kodak moment will just have to wait.

"Shit! We have to get out of here!"

I have to shout over the rolling thunder, startling myself almost as much as Mona.

"What?"

"This is what I was trying to tell—"

"This is what?"

"This is where we die!"

The thunder gets closer and closer.

"Every night, before I wake up, I dream of you and me, here, then everything goes crazy and books fly everywhere and—"

Everything goes silent, but only because it's so loud my ears just stop working, like in a dream when time slows down and your fight-or-flight response is on high alert and it feels like I've got all the time in the world to plan my next move millisecond by millisecond. But I don't.

And it feels like such a waste. It feels like seeing the future has amounted to knowing all along it wouldn't do me any good, only I realized it too late. Not even a has been, more of a never will be. Very soon to be a never was.

And I'm thinking, *Isn't my life supposed to flash before my eyes?* Yet all I can think of is how I'll never have a collection of Ferraris or a forty-acre estate or a thriving chain of coffee shops. No book deals or made-for-TV movies. No cashmere sweaters with initials on the pocket.

Now I know I'll never capitalize on this special brand of clairvoyance, never build an empire, never have a penny to leave to the children I will never have with the girl I only just met.

If you're reading this, then it's probably all that's left.

The half-empty mug sails to the floor, spewing coffee and bits of porcelain in every direction.

The lights shoot up, over the curb and slightly to the right, knocking over a fire hydrant.

Cue the slow-motion crash of a dark blue Shelby Cobra replica as it barrels through the front window of The Spy House.

All in absolute, overwhelming, total and complete reality. This time, I don't simply wake up. This time, with Mona in my arms, with senses overwhelmed, we tumble sideways and I'm rolling to shield her from the worst of it. Everything has slowed down but instead of giving me more time to react it somehow renders me a spectator to our final moments, but what else is new? The future encompasses the present; reality pierces right through the heart of the dream, and I honestly can't remember a single moment beyond the starfield of sparkling glass chasing us into that black hole.

Everything is now.

Lyrics quoted in italics are from the songs "Only" and "Every Day Is Exactly The Same" by Nine Inch Nails from the album, With Teeth. Any other song lyrics referenced or quoted in the text are entirely incidental.

PERFECT
EDGE
B O O K S

"There are many who dare not kill themselves for fear of what
the neighbours will say," Cyril Connolly wrote, and we believe
he was right.
Perfect Edge seeks books that take on the crippling fear of other
people, the question of what's correct and normal, of how life
works, of what art is.
Our authors disagree with each other; their styles vary as widely as
their concerns. What matters is the will to create books that won't be
easy to assimilate. We take risks, not for the sake of risk-taking, but for
the things that might come out of it.